INFECTION Z 3

RYAN CASEY

HBB
Higher Bank Books

The characters and events portrayed in this book are fictitious. Any similarity to real persons, living or dead, is coincidental and not intended by the author. Any reference to real locations is only for atmospheric effect, and in no way truly represents those locations.

Copyright © 2015 by Ryan Casey

Cover design by Cormar Creative

All rights reserved.

No part of this book may be reproduced in any form or by any electronic or mechanical means, including information storage and retrieval systems, without written permission from the author, except for the use of brief quotations in a book review.

Published by Higher Bank Books

If you want to be notified when Ryan Casey's next novel is released and receive an exclusive free book from his Dead Days post apocalyptic series, please sign up to his mailing list.

http://ryancaseybooks.com/fanclub

Your email address will never be shared and you can unsubscribe at any time.

INFECTION Z: 3

ONE

Holly Waterfield ran.

The taste of sweat and blood covered her lips. A crippling stitch knotted around the right side of her belly, but she couldn't give in to it—she just had to keep on pushing, keep on running away. She couldn't stop, not for anything.

The people who stopped never made it.

Holly didn't look back as she paced across the muddy field, her white dress clinging to her grimy skin with sweat and dirt. But it wasn't the sight of their mangled, distorted corpses that scared her or the sound of their raspy throats.

It was the smell. That putrid smell of decay, undeniable and unavoidable. The smell that worked its way into the linings of your nostrils and stayed there, clung on and scratched its way into your senses, permanently embedding itself into memory.

Sometimes, Holly worried whether she might miss an attack by the dead simply because she couldn't shift that damned smell out of her mind. When she went to eat, she got a whiff of that smell and it put her off her food. When she drank, she didn't taste the cool freshness of water, she just smelled the stench of death—

the smell of people she'd been with, people she'd lost. People she'd had to move on from, again and again and again.

She ran further into the darkness, into the night. The hard, frosty ground scratched at the soles of her feet, which had already been worn down by the endless running she'd had to do. She hadn't had time to put shoes on. She hadn't had time to scramble for clothes beyond her white dress. From a distance, she figured she'd look bizarre—like some kind of twisted Cinderella out of a nightmare.

Only she'd lost her beauty. She knew she'd lost her beauty, just like everyone lost their beauty in this world.

But still, she ran.

Ran across the frozen grass, past the tall, dark silhouettes of the trees, further and further away from the echoing cries and footsteps of the undead.

She thought about the people she'd lost. Adrian, Beth, Sanji. Good people. People that had helped keep her spirit and resolve right from the start of the downfall, but people she'd lost. As she ran further into the dark, the cold night enveloping its frosty arms around her, Holly wondered whether she'd outlive everybody. It was something she'd always wondered, right since losing her little sister in a road accident four years ago. She says little—she was eighteen at the time, but to a twenty-six-year-old big sister who has lived all their days of immaturity, eighteen feels practically childlike.

She remembered receiving the news that Tiff was dead. Walking the pet Bichon Frisé, Robbie, down a country lane. Land Rover hit some ice and swerved into her, killing her sister instantly (mercifully) and leaving Robbie in a painful state that only putting him to sleep could cure.

Holly sunk into a numb state of midlife—or "third-life"—crisis after that. She stopped going to work. Stopped showing up for social gatherings. Her relationship with Andy, a lovely man who was in his early thirties and inherited a fair share of wealth after the death of a close relative, crumbled to ashes, partly because he decided she wasn't enough for him and found some new model. But partly because of her distance, too. She knew that now. Accepted it.

But Holly wasn't allowed to stay in a state of misery about either of those events for long because the death of her mother from a sudden heart attack followed just weeks later.

Holly kept on running through the trees, kept on running through the darkness. The only light came from the stars that peeked through the tips of the trees and the moonlight that split through the clouds. She didn't allow fear to invade her thoughts. Not that she didn't *feel* fear—if she focused, she could drown so deep in collective fear that she'd never resurface for air—but she was good at compartmentalising fear. It was a life skill that she'd learned through her experiences, most of which had come in the last four years.

Mum, healthy Mum, out jogging and running quicker than Holly had ever dreamed of, so fit and agile and nimble, lying on the pavement clutching her chest, the paramedics pronouncing her dead at the scene.

And then there was Dad. He didn't last much longer than Mum. Six months, maybe. They say adults who have been in long-term marriages go through two kinds of reactions to the death of a loved one—they become more pro-active, or they slip even further into inactivity. It was safe to say that Dad fell firmly into the latter camp. He'd need reminding that his fridge was empty even though the sour remnants of milk in the carton told Holly he'd needed shopping for days. Subscription newspapers stacked up by the letterbox, as Dad worked his way through the news of two weeks ago, not really reading it but just staring glassy-eyed at the images, like he was playing a part in some morbid play. Holly wondered what he did when he was alone. A part of her hoped that maybe he'd spark up. Maybe he'd call an old rugby friend or pop round to a neighbour's house.

She found him dead in his favourite chair with a glass of whisky and a box of sleeping pills beside him.

It was the happiest she'd seen him for months.

She kept on running through the woods. She swore she heard noises to her left, to her right, in the darkness. The cracking of fallen branches underfoot. The whistling of trees in the wind. A crackling. A crackling, like …

She slowed down. She didn't want to stop because she knew how dangerous stopping was. But she eased her run so she could hear into the distance.

She smelled it before she heard it.

Burning. Flames.

And then the crackling of what could only be gunfire.

She heard the footsteps and the gasps following her through the trees and her body told her it was time to run again.

But before she ran, she looked down at her bare left forearm.

She looked at the bloodied bandage. Through the bandage, in her mind's eye, she could see the blood. The raw flesh like steak tartare. The tooth marks, like the piercings of a hole punch.

She looked at the bandage, and she took a deep breath and let fear fill her body for a few torturous seconds.

Remembered the dark cabin.

Remembered the burning, searing sensation of teeth ripping through her skin.

Remembered the taste of blood that filled the air.

And then she exhaled and let her fear go.

Compartmentalised.

She started running faster again, away from the zombies, through the trees and into the night.

Towards the gunfire. Towards the smoke.

Towards something new.

TWO

"You see them?"
"See them clearly."
"Yours or mine?"
"I'll take it."

A blast from Hayden's right. One second, the zombie outside the walls of Riversford Industrial Estate was there, the next second, its head exploded into a bloody firework.

Hayden pulled away from his gun and glared at Gary, who had a wide grin on his chunky face. "I said I had it," Hayden said.

Gary reloaded his rifle. "Well, actions speak louder than words. I'll let you have the next one if I'm feelin' generous."

Hayden shook his head. He couldn't deny the frustration he felt about someone else hijacking his kill. In the ten days since they'd locked down Riversford and made it their own, killing stray zombies from the safety of the rooftops had become a friendly competition. Gary, the former CityFast employee who was forever wearing the green oil-laced slacks that his old job required, was the only person who gave Hayden any real competition.

"Considerin' you've no gun trainin', you ain't so bad," Gary said, patting Hayden on his shoulder.

"I told you. Lightgun games like House of the Dead. All the training I need."

Gary chuckled and shook his head. "Who'd've thought zombie lightgun games would end up legit training?"

"Certainly not me," Hayden said. He looked out over the sunlit expanse of the wider Warrington area. Ahead of him, the icy fields were thawing out more and more gradually as January segued into February. The mornings were getting lighter, day by day, and the nights were holding off for a few extra seconds. It was still damned cold—so damned cold that Hayden had forgotten what it actually felt like to be warm—but the gentle glow of the late winter sun offered a temporary reminder as it brushed its rays against his goose-pimpled neck.

"Close your eyes and you can convince yourself it's just muck spreadin'," Gary said.

"Huh?"

Gary had his eyes closed. He was stood a few metres from the edge of the hangar, the highest point in the Riversford Industrial Estates that they'd safely locked down. He rested his rifle over his shoulders and took in a deep audible breath through his nostrils. "The smell. Completely friggin' hanging, yeah. But close your eyes and it just smells like some farmer's out spreadin' muck through the fields. All about perspective, boss. All about perspective."

Hayden knew which smell Gary was referring to. The constant stench of death and rot that lingered in the air. He wasn't a rigor mortis or decomposition expert by any means, but he knew that the bodies of the undead were rotting away right now. And as the sun rose a little earlier and set a little later every day, as the temperature ramped up and sweat replaced goose-bumps, the smell would only get worse.

Hayden closed his eyes. Took a deep breath through his nostrils. Almost heaved.

"That's bullshit."

"Cow shit, I think," Gary said, his eyes still closed. "Don't think they use bullshit to spread ... Oh. I get you now. I get you."

Hayden tutted and shook his head. "Gotta shoot, anyway. Need to speak with Matt and Karen about Tim."

"About damned time someone did," Gary said. "And who better than Sheriff McCall?"

Hayden felt his cheeks warm up. He knew Gary was taking the piss. But he had inadvertently become something of a diplomatic figure in the ten days since the Great Fire of Riversford, as he was now aptly coining it. People looked to him for answers. And sure, there were only seven of them aside from him—Sarah, Gary, Martha and Amy (Newbie's ex-wife and daughter), and a family of three: Matt, Karen and their kid, Tim. And they hadn't exactly elected Hayden leader, anything like that. But they seemed to respect him, weirdly.

And he meant "weirdly" because he couldn't remember a single time in his life when anyone outside his blood relatives came close to respecting him.

Often, even his blood relatives didn't respect his layabout ways either.

"You alright on watch?" Hayden asked.

Gary smiled and saluted. "Right as rain. Gives me a good chance to get my kill tally up anyway. Now go give that little shite a bollocking."

Hayden turned away and climbed down the ladder that crept up the side of the CityFast hangar. The bulk of the inside had been burned beyond repair, but the rusty metal ladders at the side of the building remained. There were two other bunkers, one of which they slept in. They'd locked up the CityFast hangar and boarded as many windows as they could. As Hayden descended, he heard the occasional creak inside—swore he heard a gasp or a growl. There were still zombies inside no doubt. Ones that they hadn't been able to clear out on floors that had been made inaccessible by the fire. But inaccessible to the survivors meant they were inaccessible to the zombies, too. And it wasn't a major problem. Touch wood and all that, but there couldn't be many of them in there.

They acted as a deterrent too, in a way. Just in case any larger group wandered past and fancied a piece of Riversford. They'd approach, see the burned out remains of the CityFast hangar, perhaps hear the groans of a zombie, and then they'd move on.

And if they didn't move on, they'd die.

Hayden's group would make sure of that.

Hayden climbed further down the ladders. He could hear a girl's laughter somewhere on the ground below. Amy, Newbie's daughter. Cheery, pleasant girl, ten years old. Her brown eyes were so much like her dad's that it looked like they'd been snipped out of his body and stuffed into her skull.

Which made looking into them hard. Looking into them reminded Hayden of what the group had lost. A good friend. A companion.

And remembering any kind of loss just brought the loss of Dad, of Mum, the beheading of Clarice to his mind …

Blood spurting onto the floor.

Tears rolling from her terrified eyes.

Hayden tasted copper in his mouth. His heart started to pound. His head grew dizzy, and he had to grip onto the ladder and make a conscious effort to ease his breathing.

She's gone now. She's not suffering anymore. It's okay. It's okay. Everything's okay.

Hayden reached the ground below and took a few more steadying breaths to rid the tingling nausea from his stomach. He turned and looked at the sun-soaked grounds of Riversford. There was a large parking area in front of him where the main fire had spread. Debris and charred remains had covered the ground just days ago, but they'd made a massive effort to clear it up. It wasn't easy—there were a few close calls with some of the zombies that had burned and melded with the concrete, and the stinging dust from the charred flesh of things that used to be *human beings* ... that could take its toll on a person.

Hayden walked across the concrete. The walls that they'd rebuilt towered twenty feet high around Riversford. The original metal fences had been destroyed by the mass of undead that had invaded this place ten days ago, but the group had pulled their infinite time together to use whatever loose sheets of metal, debris, rocks, and anything they could get their hands on to make something solid and sturdy. And so far, it had done the trick. It was always going to be a work in progress—as was everything nowadays—but it was a start.

"Hi, Hayden!"

Amy's voice brought a shiver through Hayden's body. He forced his best smile and turned to look at her. "Hi, Amy. You okay?"

She was wearing a red hoodie and ripped trackie bottoms. She had that look that everyone had nowadays; the bags under the eyes, the chapped lips, the bony physique. She looked at Hayden with those eyes that could so easily have been her dad's and she nodded. "Fine. Just ... just playing around."

Her gaze dropped to the ground, and Hayden knew right away that she was hiding something.

"Seen Tim anywhere?" Hayden asked.

Amy lifted her head and shook it way too enthusiastically. She held her hands together in front of her, slumped her shoulders. "No, I haven't seen him. If he's doing something wrong, I ... I haven't seen him."

Hayden was about to say something in return to Amy when he caught sight of movement in the corner of his left eye.

When he saw what it was—who it was—his insides burned.

"That little shit ..."

Hayden rushed past Amy towards the wall. Tim was a quarter of the way up it. He looked back at the ground with fear on his face. His arm was caught underneath a loose piece of rubble.

"I didn't know he was there!" Amy shouted. "I swear I didn't know he was there."

But Hayden disregarded her. He ran towards the wall and ran towards Tim.

Kids. Frigging annoying kids. Who needed them anyway?

THREE

"Ah, you've got to understand how it is, mate. Kids will be kids."

Matt Striker wasn't the easiest man to deal with. It didn't help that his wife, Karen, rolled her eyes and did an annoying little laugh whenever Hayden pulled them up about their wayward son, Tim, either. They were the kind of parents Hayden despised—parents who let their kids run wild and made no attempt to keep them under control. He thought the zombie apocalypse might wean down on those kinds of parents, but meeting Matt and Karen soon changed his mind on that front.

Hayden swallowed a lump in his dry throat as he stood near the door to the second hangar, the one they used as a living quarters now. Matt and Karen were opposite him, pottering about washing clothes in icy cold water, the smell of sweat strong in the air. Matt was in his forties or fifties, with grey hair that looked slicked back even in times of crisis. He was dressed in a white shirt and black trousers like he'd just stepped out of a business meeting and into the end of the world. His wife, Karen, had shoulder length dark hair and looked like she'd been a little on the skinny side even before the world went tits up. She was constantly smiling though. End of the world and a smile was always etched on her face. Hayden admired that. But what he didn't admire was the way they let their kid run amok.

"I'm not saying kids can't be kids," Hayden said, keeping as cool as possible while Matt and Karen continued to potter around. "I'm just saying we have to be more ... more careful. The world we live in right now, it's different to—to how it used to be."

"And you think we don't know that?" Matt said. There was never venom in his voice or malice in his grey-green eyes, but Hayden could sense the frustration bubbling underneath. Like banter gone awry.

Another deep breath of the cold but stuffy air. "Not accusing you of anything. I just—"

"Tim's always been hard work," Karen said, wiping her damp hands on her grey jogging bottoms. "Right from being a baby. Used to moan all through the night. Tried to stop it but to be honest, some kids are just wired up that way. He's a decent kid at heart though."

"And I don't doubt that," Hayden said. He wasn't one for conflict, but he could feel the adrenaline surging through his body and prompting him to fight. "He seems a good kid. But he can't go wandering—"

"You don't have kids, do you?" Matt asked.

Hayden closed his mouth. Shook his head.

"Or siblings? You don't have any younger ... Oh. Sorry. I really didn't ..."

The words cut into Hayden's body and, at that point, he couldn't help himself.

"I just dragged your boy down from the frigging wall," Hayden said, arms shaking and palms sweating. "I just pulled him down from the wall we've put sweat and blood into building this last ten days. So excuse me if I'm a bit agitated or if what I'm saying goes against your idea of raising a kid, but I'm just being careful, that's all. Now can you please just keep a closer frigging eye on your son?"

Hayden could tell from the silence that followed his outburst that maybe, just maybe, he'd crossed a little too far over the line. Matt stared at him with puzzled eyes. Karen's smile dropped. They both looked at him like they were seeing him for the first time, seeing the real Hayden with all his walls and defences broken down, looking inside his soul.

Hayden tensed his fists and looked at the tiled floor in front of him. "I'm sorry. I just—"

"No," Matt said, an assertiveness to his voice that Hayden wasn't used to hearing. He rubbed his hands together and walked towards Hayden. "I understand. You have a problem and you've aired it. I appreciate your honesty. We appreciate your honesty."

Hayden couldn't help but feel shitty at how damned reasonable Matt was being about his outburst. He struggled to focus on Matt's eyes so he kept the most of his focus on the brown shoes on Matt's feet. "I shouldn't have spoken to you like—"

Matt placed a heavy hand on his shoulder. The dampness from his palms spread through his coat. It was a gesture that forced Hayden to lift his head, to look Matt right in his eyes. Hayden could see his eyes were bloodshot. He was half-smiling. A genuine smile of appreciation. Respect. "You're looking out for our boy. You're stressed. We're all stressed. Sorry we couldn't keep him more ... more under control. But we appreciate what you do, Hayden."

"We really do," Karen said. But her smile was too wide, too false to take seriously. Hayden knew it, Matt knew it, and Hayden knew that Matt knew he knew it and vice versa.

Okay, cutting through the complicated way of putting it: Karen could be a bit of a bitch where other people were concerned.

"I'll have a word with Tim when we eat later. Hear Martha's cooking up a delicious—"

"Wait," Hayden said, lifting a hand. "Let me guess. Baxter's Chicken Soup?"

Matt patted Hayden's shoulder. His half-smile widened into a full one, and it was as if the confrontation that occurred just moments ago had faded into distant memory. "Tomato soup and ready-packed toast, fresh from the dusty, damp cellar. Featuring cobwebs and rat shit."

"Sounds delicious," Hayden said, his stomach turning in the complete opposite reaction to hunger.

Matt chuckled and returned to his wife's side, grabbing a soaked shirt from the icy cold water basin and rinsing it out. Later, they'd start a fire and dry out the clothes over it. Laundry, cooking—the Riversford group were a well-oiled machine. They'd made serious progress in the last ten days. There was still something dreamlike about it all, though. Like they were just playing house and someone was going to appear out of thin air and rescue them from this eternal struggle. The fantasy.

There was the knowledge, too. The knowledge that this place wouldn't last forever simply because it *couldn't* last forever. No place lasted forever. Something would happen. Something would lead the group astray like they were destined to be led for the rest of their aimless lives. And it was strange, for Hayden, because he realised now just how similar his life was before the rise of the undead to now. Life really was just an endless loop of waking and drinking and eating and smoking and video-gaming and napping and takeaway-ing and …

On and on and on, without an end goal, without direction.

And sure, he didn't have video games anymore, but in terms of profession he was as much a layabout as he used to be.

But the beauty of his old life was that he could live without direction through choice. He had the option to live some other way, but he chose a life of booze and weed.

Now he had no choice but to sit around and do fuck all, he wanted something else. He wanted to see the world. He wanted to stand at the top of the Rockefeller building and look out over Central Park on a gorgeous, blue-skied day like he'd seen in so many movies. He wanted to step inside the Coliseum in Rome and feel the adrenaline kick of a million spectators before him.

He wanted to *live*.

Instead, he was being forced to survive.

"I should head off, anyway," Hayden said. "See you for food in ..." He started to say "in an hour," but he knew how futile the suggestion of time was now. Sure, the clocks kept on ticking and the days kept on turning. But eventually the batteries would stop. Calendars would rot, just like bodies. Time would go on, but human perception of it wouldn't.

"See you for food when we smell it," Matt said, a chuckle in his voice.

Hayden nodded. "When we smell it."

He turned away from Matt and Karen and stepped out of the hangar.

When he saw Sarah standing in front of him, he knew from the whitewashed look on her face that something was wrong.

He knew from the glassiness of her bright blue eyes that something terrible had happened.

"What—"

"You need to see this, Hayden," Sarah said, her voice shaky and quivery. "You—you need to see this."

It was only then that he saw the blood on her hands.

FOUR

In the three weeks since the start of the outbreak, Hayden McCall had seen a lot of horrifying things.
But few things unsettled him more than what he saw in the yard outside the hangar.

The first thing he saw was Amy, Martha and Newbie's daughter. At first, Hayden thought she was smiling or laughing like she always seemed to be.

But when he looked closer, he saw the tears rolling down her cheeks. Her bloodshot eyes. Snot dripping from the end of her nose like a leaky tap.

There was a complete stillness to the grounds of Riversford as Sarah led Hayden outside. A stillness, a complete silence but for the cawing of birds, the scraping of tree branches in the breeze, and the shakiness of Sarah's breaths. The moment Hayden saw the blood on her hands, he knew something was wrong. He knew some kind of accident had happened.

That accident lay on the concrete six metres away from him.

Tim's body was completely rigid. In fact, it was so rigid that he looked like he was playing a game of musical statues. His right arm was pointing up into the air, his fingers twisted like he was reaching out for something way beyond his grasp. His eyes were wide open—really wide, wider than any eyes Hayden had ever seen. And as Hayden stepped closer, as Sarah's shaky breaths became sniffs and Amy's sobs grew louder, Hayden noticed the paleness of Tim's skin. His cheeks were a pasty yellow colour, but thick blue bruises under his eyes contrasted it like the difference between day and night.

And then there was the blood. The blood that had streamed out of his nose, his ears, his mouth. His black hair was caked with sweat and grease. His white v-neck T-shirt was covered in so much blood that it looked like Tim must've had some kind of accident with paint.

Hayden stepped over him. His mouth was dry and tasteless. He stared down at Tim's body and a lump welled up in his throat. He couldn't speak. He couldn't understand. All he could think of, his heartbeat pumping gradually faster, was how this had to be one of Tim's infuriating little pranks. He'd been alive. Less than an hour ago, Hayden had climbed up the wall of debris and dragged him down. He'd had a stern word with him, then gone inside and spoken to his parents.

And now he was ...

"Is he—is he dead?" Amy spluttered, tears dripping onto the dusty ground beneath.

Hayden crouched down beside Tim. Tim's body was so cold that Hayden didn't even have to touch it to know there wasn't an ounce of life left inside. But he reached for Tim's wrist, and then for his neck. He held his hand there in hope that this was all just some kind of messed up joke; all some kind of nightmare that he was going to wake up from soon, like the nightmare he had about his dead family biting one another and laughing and gasping and ...

"He's gone," Hayden said.

He stood up. Wiped his eyes with his sleeve and looked back down at Tim. He couldn't shift his eyes from him. He couldn't understand. Something had happened. Some kind of accident had to have happened.

"Oh no no no," Amy said, crying more freely now. Her sobbing turned to wailing, and soon Gary and Martha emerged from their respective hangars and came running over to see what the hell was wrong.

"Shit!" Gary said, stumbling when he saw Tim's body lying on the ground. He backed away a little, and the colour seeped from his cheeks. "What's ... what's ..."

"Amy?" Martha said, running up to her daughter and wrapping her arms around her. She was a curvy woman who looked older than the forties she was in. Her hair was dark and frizzy, and she always wore a navy blue coat and khaki jeans that looked a couple of sizes too skinny for her. "What's happened?" she asked, clutching the back of her daughter's head and staring wide-eyed at Tim's body. "What ... Is he ..."

"I don't know what happened," Sarah said. Her speech was slurred, distant, like she couldn't catch up with her railroad of thoughts. "I—I just came out here. Saw him on the ground next—next to Amy."

"What happened, Amy?" Martha asked, pushing her daughter away and rubbing up and down her arms. "Tell your mum. What happened?"

Amy sobbed some more. "He—he just fell. We—we were playing and he just fell."

She descended into more tears.

Hayden didn't like the way Amy said that Tim "just fell." He was a kid, only nine or ten years old. And sure, they didn't exactly have the luxury of three nutritious meals a day here, but he was a healthy kid who did a lot of running about.

Hayden found his gaze drifting to the blood that had drooled out of Tim's eyes, nose, ears, mouth. But it was Tim's eyes that he found himself settling on. That terrified look in his eyes, and the way he was holding his hand into the air as if to grab something.

Or push something away.

"Some kind of—of seizure or somethin'?" Gary asked.

Hayden just shook his head. He couldn't suggest anything because he didn't know what had happened. Just that one second, Tim was alive and the next, he was dead.

"What if—what if it's a virus?" Martha said, panic creeping into her voice as she clutched her crying daughter. "What if something's spreading? Something—something different to the undead?"

"We don't know anything for sure," Hayden said. The voice came from somewhere deep within, a part that he wasn't in control of. He brushed back his sweaty hair. "We ... we just need to find out if ..."

His voice drifted away and his stomach turned.

Matt and Karen.

They weren't out here.

They didn't know yet.

Gary edged forward towards Tim's body. "I'll take him somewhere more sightly—"

"Don't touch him," Hayden said. "We don't know if there is some kind of virus, but we can't take any chances just yet."

"So we just leave him here on the ground for his mum and dad to find?" Gary said.

"I ... I've got his blood on my hands," Sarah said.

Hayden and the others all looked at her. She held her bloody hands up, which quivered and shook.

"I ... I got his blood on my hands. So if there's a virus, I ..."

Sarah didn't get to finish what she was starting to say because she must've heard exactly what Hayden heard.

Footsteps.

Hayden turned around. At the hangar door, he saw Matt and Karen emerge. Karen had that forced half-smile on her face like always, and Matt was wiping some suds on his white shirt. He frowned at the group; looked at them with confusion and then bewilderment and then, all of a sudden, fear.

Fear, as his eyes drifted from Hayden to Gary and then to Sarah, Sarah with blood on her hands.

Fear, as Amy sobbed her eyes out.

Fear, as he saw the body on the ground.

Hayden took a deep breath in and stepped towards Matt and Karen. "You two don't want to—"

But Matt barged past him, and then he barged past Gary and the others and when he saw his son's body lying there on the ground, Hayden actually saw the muscles in his face drop.

"Not my boy," he said, lifting his son's rigid body up, lips quivering. "Not—not my boy. Please not my boy."

Karen's fake smile dropped.

She fell to her knees beside her husband, beside her dead son.

And in the glow of the late winter sun, she let out a scream that Hayden would never forget for the rest of his life, however long that was.

FIVE

"No. You aren't taking our boy away from us. You—you aren't taking our boy away from us."

Hayden leaned against the door to Matt and Karen's room. It was a small, six by six-metre space in the confines of one of the abandoned Riversford hangars that the group had occupied. There were three sleeping bags laid out on the floor. Hayden felt a great sadness when he saw the bump in the little blue sleeping bag. Karen crouched beside it, cuddled up to it, throaty cries creeping out of her throat. She stroked her hands against the sleeping bag, stroked from head to toe and back again.

Blood seeped through the blue cover.

Matt stood in Hayden's way. He glared at him with bloodshot red eyes. Hayden could smell the sweat coming from his body. The sweat that always came with shock. "Please. Just—just leave us in peace with our son. Leave us in peace."

Hayden felt his insides turn. "I ... I want that but—"

"Then you'll walk away right now and leave us to mourn. You've lost people too. You ... you have no idea how we feel right now, but you've lost people too. So you know what—what we have to do."

Hayden felt deep sympathy for Matt and Karen. Sure, Tim could be a bit of a handful, but weren't all kids a bit of a handful from time to time?

The way he'd dropped dead. "Just fell," as Amy put it. One second, alive, the next, bleeding out of his orifices on the ground.

Hayden thought too about Sarah. About her fears of this being some kind of virus. "We can't be sure your son's body is … is safe."

Matt squared up to Hayden. "I told you to—"

"Did Tim ever have any … any funny turns? Seizures, things like that?"

Matt ground his teeth together. His cheeks flushed, and it looked for a moment as if he was going to lash out at Hayden just like Hayden had lashed out at him earlier.

"No," he said. He wiped the sweat from the side of his head. "I … No. He was healthy. Good at … at PE." He chuckled. "Little champion at the egg and spoon race. My little champion."

His voice faltered at those final words, and once again the guilt welled up inside Hayden.

"I'm sorry," Hayden said. "I … Really. I'm so sorry this happened."

"We'll get who did this to you," Karen mumbled, stroking her son's body and sniffing back her tears. "We'll get who did this to you."

It was at that moment that Hayden's understanding and perspective shifted. Karen's words—we'll get who did this to you. She was suggesting murder. Foul play. "Karen, I don't think anyone murdered—"

"What the fuck do you know?" Karen spat. She looked up at Hayden with dagger-like eyes. It was the most honest look Hayden thought he'd seen from Karen since meeting her.

"I ... I'm just saying. I think it's more likely we're dealing with—"

"Are you a doctor? Are you a medical professional? Are—are you in any way qualified to tell me what's—what's right and wrong for my son? For my little boy?"

"Karen," Matt cut in.

"No," Karen shouted. She stood up and walked towards Hayden. "I won't have this. I won't have this." She smacked a hand hard against Hayden's chest. "People thinking they can tell me how to raise my son, how to look after my son. People ... people still telling me what to do even when he's gone."

She lashed out and hit harder and then, exhausted, she fell crying into her husband's arms.

Matt gave Hayden a look that told him everything he needed to hear—it was time to leave.

"I just want my boy back," Karen sobbed. "I ... I just want my little boy back."

Hayden wanted to tell Karen that he understood loss, that he'd lost so much in his life that he could relate. But a part of him was numb to loss. A part of him was desensitised. Since Clarice died in front of him, he hadn't cried about her. He hadn't mourned, not in the traditional ways. He'd banished the memories from his mind. And they came crawling back to him in the confines of sleep when he couldn't run away, but in reality he just kept his eyes shut to the truth and powered on with life.

He couldn't allow himself to grieve. He couldn't allow himself to *feel*. He'd felt way too much in his life, and it had caught up with him one time too many.

He turned away from Matt and Karen's room and left them to grieve. He'd give them time. One more night with their son, and then they'd have to clear their heads and step forward with the only logical thing: burial. It wasn't a nice thought. It was a damned horrid thought. But they had a chance to bury their son.

Not a lot of people had a chance to say a proper goodbye to their loved ones in this world. That was something.

Hayden pushed open the rusty metal door that led out into the Riversford grounds. He zipped up his thick winter coat as the cold of night surrounded him. His breath frosted from his mouth as he walked across the concrete, past the spot where they'd found Tim's body, and towards the wall. Sarah was up there on watch. He had to go up there, reassure her everything was going to be okay. She'd been pretty shaken up by Tim's death. All of them had.

He climbed the ladder up the side of the CityFast hangar and reached the roof. He liked coming up here at night. Night watch was his favourite because it gave him a legitimate reason to avoid sleep.

He walked across the stones laid on the roof and towards Sarah, who sat at the edge of the building with her eye to the rifle scope.

"Hey," Hayden said.

Sarah jumped, lowered the weapon and swung to look at him. "Damn. You love giving me a fright, don't you?"

Hayden perched down beside her and she looked through her scope again. "Figured you could use some company."

"I'm not sure what I need right now," Sarah said. Her voice still had that distant shakiness to it like it had down in the yard when they'd found Tim's body. "This. Everything. It's all just so ..."

"Shitty?" Hayden said.

"Shitty," Sarah said. She lowered the scope and together with Hayden, stared out at the fields and the trees beyond.

"I just keep thinking of Tim and wondering how this world can be so damned cruel," she said.

Hayden took the gun from her and put his eye to the scope. "If you're only just realising that, then poor you."

He looked out beyond the wall. Saw the empty streets, the still, abandoned houses, the vacant fields, the vast forest.

"You seem so ... so calm. About everything. Hayden, you haven't once spoken to me about what happened to Clarice."

The words made Hayden's grip on the gun tighten. He felt his cheeks heating up, his mouth drying. "There's nothing to say. She's ... she's dead. She died and she's gone. Nothing more to be done."

"But it's okay to talk, sometimes," Sarah said. "It's better to talk sometimes. I know how close she was to you. And I can't imagine how much it must tear you up inside."

No, you can't imagine, Hayden thought. You can't imagine and nobody can imagine. Not even I can imagine because if I imagine I see evil; evil that I can never unsee. "I'm okay," he said, forcing the words through his tight lips. "I'll ..."

And then he saw the movement in the fields.

Saw the woman sprinting in the direction of Riversford.

Cream dress. Dark hair. Fear on her face.

"What's up?" Sarah asked.

"There's—there's a woman out there."

Hayden kept on staring at the woman. A part of him thought she looked so ragged and pale that she had to be a zombie. But no—she was muttering something. *Shouting* something, even. Words that were becoming clearer. Words that made sense.

"Help me!" she screamed. "Let me in! Help me! Please!"

Hayden was about to lower the gun when he saw the movement behind her.

The crowd of zombies closing in, one by one ...

SIX

"No. No chance. It's too risky."

Sarah shook her head. Hayden could see from the way the colour was returning to her face in the glow of the moonlight that she wasn't happy with him. "She's out there on her own. She needs help. What are we supposed to do? Just leave her out there to die?"

Hayden looked back through the rifle scope over the wall at the scene Sarah was referring to. The woman in the white dress running for her life, shouting for help. And behind her, getting closer and closer, a crowd of a dozen zombies.

"We can take a few of them out," Hayden said. "Snipe a few zombies from here and give her a chance. But she isn't coming inside. Not with ... with what happened. To Tim."

"Is that the real reason you're not letting her inside? Or is the real reason just that you're too damned afraid to let *anyone* inside anymore?"

Hayden tightened his grip on the rifle, eased his aim and pointed at the zombies behind the woman. He fired a shot, sent it slicing right through the zombie's shoulder but not quite hitting the neck. "This isn't about—"

"Get real, Hayden. You've not been the same since Clarice died, and it's about time you started facing up to it. Remember the man who went back into the CityFast HQ ten days ago? The man who went back and saved the people who we're living with right now? The people we're looking after?"

Hayden fired another bullet in the direction of the zombies. He heard footsteps as someone clambered up the ladder, probably Gary. "I let them down. I let ... I let Matt and Karen down."

"And you're about to let somebody else down if you don't come to your frigging senses and let that woman in. At least give her a chance, Hayden. Let's—let's monitor her, at least. But don't leave her out there to die. Don't make that call. I ... I won't let you make that call."

Hayden glanced away from his scope and met Sarah's eyes. He saw that look. That look of disdain, but also a look of fear. A look that told Hayden she didn't trust him, couldn't predict what he was going to do, anymore. And in a way, it echoed Hayden's own thoughts. He wasn't sure if he could trust himself. He wasn't sure whether he'd be able to trust anyone or anything ever again.

"The hell's goin' on down there?" Gary asked. He walked over to the edge of the hangar and joined Sarah and Hayden in looking over the wall.

"There's a woman out there," Sarah said.

"A ... A live one?"

"Not for long if Hayden has his way."

Hayden looked back through the scope. The woman was just metres away from the wall now. They could—*could*—go down there and throw the rope ladder over for her. But it was a risk. There was a chance of the visible zombies being a smaller splinter group of a larger herd, the like of which Hayden hadn't seen since that fateful night ten days ago. And the group couldn't suffer another upheaval. Not so hot on the heels of Tim's death.

The thought hit him in its rawest form: Tim is dead. Gone. Finished.

"So what do we do?" Gary asked. "Out there 'n help her or—"

"It's too risky. It's too risky."

"Of course it's too frigging risky," Sarah said, frustration bubbling through her voice. "Everything's frigging risky these days. But we have to take risks. You've seen that yourself. We take risks or we die. That's all life is now. One risk after another."

Hayden fired at another of the zombies. The bullet fizzed past it, missed it completely. The zombies were gaining ground on the woman, who was right up to the wall now, scratching at the stones and shouting out.

"Screw this," Gary said. "I ain't leavin' her out there to squeal."

"Amen to that," Sarah said, heading for the ladder.

"How does she know?"

Gary clambered down the ladder first, Sarah following shortly behind. The sound of the woman's screams echoed through the night.

"Know what?" Sarah asked.

Hayden looked back through his scope at the oncoming zombies. He got one in his sights, tickled the trigger, but this time he didn't fire. "How does she know there's someone here to help her?"

Sarah didn't respond.

She was already down the ladder, running towards the gates.

Hayden watched Gary and Sarah appear to his lower right. All the while, the zombies edged closer. He saw Sarah and Gary climb up the debris that Tim had climbed, scamper up to the top of it like rats in a scrapyard, and then when they reached the top they lowered the rope ladder and shouted out for the woman to grab on.

Hayden fired at the nearest zombie.

And then at the one behind.

And the one behind that.

But every time he fired, he felt something welling deep within.

Like he was making an error of judgement. Like they were all opening themselves up to a new set of horrors.

Paranoia? Probably.

But paranoia had served him well so far.

He watched Gary and Sarah fish the rope ladder further down towards the woman. Saw the sides of it strain under her weight as she clutched onto the bottom of it, invisible to Hayden but there for the mind's eye to see. He watched Gary and Sarah hold on even tighter as the woman ascended, as the remaining zombies got closer, closer …

He pointed at the zombies and he pulled the trigger.

Nothing happened.

No explosion from the end of the gun.

Nothing.

Fuck.

He lowered the gun. Went to reload, but it was jammed. He looked through the scope. Looked over at the ladder. The zombies would be on her if he didn't kill them fast. They'd be …

He saw the woman climbing up onto the wall, her arms over Sarah and Gary's shoulders.

Hayden felt a simultaneous hit of relief and disappointment. And that reactionary sense of disappointment absolutely terrified him.

He lowered the gun completely and headed down the ladder to the yard. He had to meet this woman. Make sure she wasn't going to cause trouble. Make sure she could be trusted.

If anyone could be trusted.

He saw her sitting on the concrete, tears rolling down her cheeks, lit up by the dim glow of Gary's torchlight.

Hayden walked slowly towards her. Sarah and Gary were still, in a daze, like they'd received some bad news.

And Hayden understood the bad news the moment the woman pulled back the bandage on her left forearm, revealing a gaping bite wound.

His stomach sank. And rose.

And terrified him.

He walked up to her. She was bitten. No arguing. No denying. What had to be done, had to be done.

"She was bit," Gary said, shaking his head. But he didn't look disappointed. He looked amazed.

"We need to talk about—"

"She was bit over a week ago," Sarah said.

Hayden narrowed his eyes. "That's not possible. She … she can't …"

"I was bitten ten days ago," the woman said, looking right up at Hayden. "And I'm … I'm still here."

And then she passed out and hit the concrete.

SEVEN

The woman's name was Holly Waterfield.

She lay back against a plumped-up cushion in a spare room in the living quarters. Her dark hair was so sweaty that it looked plastered to her head. The dress she was wearing looked like it might have been white once upon a time, a long time ago.

Right now, it was a discoloured cream shade, a combination of sweat, dirt and blood laced through it.

On her left forearm, the exposed remains of a bite wound.

She opened her eyes when Hayden entered the room. It was night now, deep in the night, and although Hayden and the others had agreed to give her some rest, it was important to monitor this woman. Hayden couldn't shake the feeling that she might have something to do with Callum's old Riversford group; the ones who had fled this place. It was unlikely, sure, but there was no way of being certain how anyone was going to operate in this new world.

She stared intently at his face with her brown eyes. Deep purple bags were wrapped around the outside of them, like bruises from a punch.

"Hope you don't mind me disturbing you," Hayden said, keeping the metal door slightly ajar so he could still feel the cool silence of the corridor. He didn't want to completely commit to being in this room alone with this woman. He didn't want to risk anything.

Holly yawned and stretched out her arms. "It's okay. Wasn't sleeping too good anyway."

"You looked like you were sleeping just fine."

"Do you always watch strangers sleep?"

Hayden went to respond, but he felt his cheeks heating up.

Holly shook her head. "Sorry. I shouldn't tease. Just ... just being out there on my own for so long. I've missed people."

Hayden nodded. A part of him wanted to walk closer to her, create a wider sphere of trust. But he held back. Stayed by the door. He didn't want to get suckered in. He had no idea who to trust, what to believe, not after all the loss the misplaced trust of the group had caused already.

"You can say it," Holly said. "This is an interrogation. You don't trust me. I can understand that."

Hayden was amazed at Holly's apparent ability to read his thoughts. "This isn't an interrog—"

"Come on, man. A spade's a spade these days. It's better if we're just up front and honest. Lies don't get anyone anywhere anymore."

Hayden wished that was true.

"You say you were out there. Alone. How long for?"

Holly puffed out her plump lips. "About ten days. Group I was with got attacked. Nothing I could do for them."

"You were bit ten days ago?"

Holly looked down at her arm and a paleness swept across her face. "Yeah. That happened about ten days ago. I was fleeing the cottage I was holed up in. Sprinting through some woods when one of the bastards attacked me. Thought I was a goner. Funny how things work out."

She smiled at Hayden. Hayden didn't have a clue how to read it.

He conjured up the courage to step a little further into the room. It felt warmer in here than it did out in the corridor. He could taste the sweat in the air, thick and muggy. "What brought you here?"

Holly scratched at her bare shins and shrugged. "Luck, I guess. I was staying in a cabin in those woods across for a while. And then ... then something chased me in there."

"Zombies?"

"Dunno," Holly said, shaking her head. "Animal of some kind. Or animals. Maybe zombies. Maybe people. It was dark. I couldn't be sure. But anyway. I got freaked, I ran. And I guess I'm lucky I ended up here."

Hayden tried to keep his body language as calm and unrevealing as possible. "Were you watching us?"

"Watching you?"

"When we first saw you. You were running at this place screaming for help. Like you knew someone was in here. Were you watching us?"

Holly shook her head. She had a pretty face, really. Her brown eyes glowed in the candlelight. "You're an untrusting man, aren't you?"

"You'd be untrusting too if you'd been through the things we've been through."

Holly tilted her head like she was weighing up Hayden's words. "I heard the gunshots and smelled the smoke ten days ago. The day the bite happened. I thought about approaching you, but then I figured a place firing bullets and burning shit wasn't a place I wanted to just waltz into out of the blue. Saw you rebuilding the walls, saw you popping biter brains. Bitta caution comes in handy every now and then. But anyway, I figured you'd be moving on when you heard."

Hayden frowned. "When we heard what?"

Holly looked at him through narrowed eyes. "You haven't heard the transmission?"

Just hearing the word "transmission" made Hayden's skin crawl. The last transmission led him here. Led Newbie to his death. Led Clarice to her execution. "What transmission?"

Holly whistled. "Wow. You really have been living the Amish life. When I was with my last group, we heard a transmission. Some freak signal broke through to a guy called Harry's mobile. There was news on there. News about extraction points. One of them's in Holyhead."

Hayden shook his head. "You heard a signal? That's impossible."

"I've no reason to bullshit."

"Then why didn't you ... why didn't you follow it?"

Holly smiled and raised her left forearm. "The second anyone saw this, I thought I knew what they'd do to me. Everyone knows what they'd do to me. And hell, I guess I gave up when shit went down in my last group. Resigned myself to just—just making it on my own. And then I bumped into you people, and I'm starting to wonder if maybe there's a chance."

Hayden saw the glimmer in Holly's eyes. And although it didn't *feel* like her story added up—although the talk of signals and transmissions and a ten day old bite seemed impossible—here she was, alive, talking to him with a bite wound and showing no signs of turning.

"A chance of what?" Hayden asked.

Holly leaned forward. "A chance to go to Holyhead. To get the hell out of here. And ... and to take me with you."

Hayden shook his head and stepped back. "We've got a good place here. We can't take any more risks. And what's to stop whoever's there just executing you like you worried about in the first place?"

"Maybe so," Holly said, her voice raspy. "Maybe they will just shoot me on sight. Maybe my gut's right and maybe you're right.

But you let me in. I didn't ... I didn't expect you to let me in, but you did. Even after seeing my frigging wound, you let me in. Gave me a pillow to sleep on. My own frigging *room*. So I dunno. Call it a revival of faith. Something like that."

Hayden pondered Holly's words. She'd been bitten ten days ago and she was still alive. There was some kind of extraction point on the Holyhead coast.

But all this talk of transmissions and signals ... He couldn't take another risk. Not again.

"We'll sleep on it," Hayden said, with no intention to even debate Holly's proposals. Way too risky. They couldn't just sacrifice all the good work they'd done on the minuscule chance of hope.

"Please do," Holly said. "Because ... not to blow my own trumpet, but I've not met anyone else bit who hasn't, like, turned. So yeah. Maybe they will just shoot me like I thought all along. But maybe there'll be someone who sees beyond the bite. Someone who sees ... I dunno. Potential, or whatever. Don't you see that?"

Hayden walked back to the door. He smiled and nodded at Holly. "Get some rest. We'll speak again tomorrow."

Holly looked back at him with those glistening eyes. Beyond the grease and the sweat, he saw a hidden beauty. "I'm not going anywhere," she said.

Hayden closed the door and stepped out into the dark silence of the hangar corridor.

A transmission. An extraction point.

A cure?

He shook his head. Walked down the corridor towards his room.

Faint hope had cost him too much already.

He wasn't putting anyone else at risk. Not now. Not ever.

But a tiny voice in the corner of his mind whispered, "what if? What if?"

And as Hayden lay down his head and closed his eyes, he saw

the person behind the voice. Saw Holly's glistening brown eyes, her seductive smile, all the time repeating the same two words again and again.

What if?

What if?

EIGHT

Matt sat on the edge of the bed and stared down at his still wife, his even stiller son.

Karen had been sleeping for a while now. She'd laid beside Tim and wrapped her arms around his cooling body. And he knew it was wrong. He knew it was damned wrong, and he knew how weird it might look to other people, other people who hadn't lost a son like them, other people who didn't understand.

But Karen needed her time with their boy. She needed her time to grieve in her own way.

Matt needed his time, too.

He leaned back against the wall and stared up at the ceiling. The cream paint was fading away. Mould was gathering in the top corners. It was something Matt had never noticed before. Something he'd been too overwhelmed by the positivity of the new world that Hayden and the others allowed his family to live in to even think of noticing.

But he saw it now. Saw it clearly. Thick black mould spreading across the corners of the room, swallowing it up from within with its endless darkness.

He closed his eyes and took a shaky breath. There was a lingering sour smell in the air, and Matt knew exactly what it was. He'd smelt it before when his Uncle Jim, a mortician, let him down in the mortuary one warm summer afternoon. As a six-year-old Matt walked past the endless stacks of bodies, tags attached to the toes, the one thing he'd never forget was that awful smell of sourness. Not strong, but subtle, like off-milk left to warm up in the next door neighbour's window.

But he knew the smell. He recognised the smell and he smelled it again right now, and that just brought the reality home to Matt.

Tim's gone. My boy's gone. He's dead and gone and he ain't ever coming back.

He listened to the sound of his own raspy breaths rising and falling. In his right ear, a slight drone of tinnitus that he'd developed ten days ago when one of the bastards holding his family and him hostage blasted a gun right beside him. It seemed such a minor problem at the time. It kept him awake at night, but it was something he told himself he'd get used to. Something he'd adapt to.

But now, he felt the volume of the drone creeping up a decibel, felt it scratching at the side of his skull and threatening to rip his brain out of its shell.

Tim's gone he's gone you lost him you loser lost him gone gone gone.

Matt cleared his throat to shift the sound of the drone, even just for a split second. His throat was raw and dry. He couldn't remember the last time he'd had a drink or anything to eat, for that matter. He'd tried to eat some of the tomato soup Martha had made earlier, but the tanginess of it just made him want to puke.

And the redness. Rich, thick red, like blood.

Like the blood on Tim's face.

Dripping out of his nostrils.

His eyes.

Bloodshot red.

Terrified.

Matt shook his head again. He could feel his heart picking up. He had to pull himself together. He had to be strong, for Karen. Karen was struggling. She was down there on the floor holding their fucking dead son while Matt just sat back on the bed and ... and did what?

Nothing, as always. Nothing at all. You lost him. He's dead. He's—

"Karen," Matt mumbled. But it was more to break the barrage of his own thoughts than anything.

He listened for a response.

Nothing.

He didn't say her name again. Couldn't bring himself to wake her up. She needed time. He'd be cruel to deny her that. And sure, it was wrong clinging on to their dead boy like she was. But those rules of right and wrong were made in the old world. The world where other people decided what was right and what was wrong based on their own messed up ideas of how society should be. Things were different now. It was rare that a mother got a chance to lay next to her boy, to say a final goodbye to him. Merciful, almost. Cause Matt had seen what happened to most of the kids Tim's age. Bites all over their necks. Stuffing their faces in the family dog, and the dog's sad eyes looking up and wondering what in the hell they'd done to deserve such a betrayal.

It was peaceful to give Tim a goodbye like this. Different. Precious.

So Matt opened his eyes and pulled himself to the edge of the bed. He'd be damned if he didn't get a chance to kiss his boy on the head one last time, stroke his dark, curly hair, hold him and Karen and pretend they were back at home on a Sunday morning when Tim used to hop in with them and they'd all just lay there, all sweet and perfect and together.

He reached the edge of the bed and he saw Karen move.

"I was just coming down there," Matt said, and he realised

then just how weak his voice was; how damned wiped out he sounded.

Karen looked at him. And at first, Matt thought he saw complete sadness and grief in her bloodshot eyes. They were so red. Red like he'd never seen.

And then he saw the blood drooling from her lips and he knew something was wrong.

"Karen? What's …"

But Matt trusted his wife enough to allow her to stand.

Allow her to throw herself at him.

And when he started struggling, when he understood what was happening, he was already too late.

He felt Karen's teeth stab the left side of his neck, heard his flesh tearing like scissors through a chicken fillet. And then he felt the blood. The warm spray of blood that fountained from the point of agony on the side of his neck covered his wife's hair, covered the bed, covered the sleeping bag that his dead son lay under.

As Matt struggled to the edge of the bed, his wife scratching and snapping at him, he saw his son's eyes staring up into nothingness. His body was still, his eyes were vacant. There wasn't a glimmer of life in him.

Or a glimmer of undead.

And then he felt another bite sink into his left shoulder and he knew it was over.

NINE

Hayden woke suddenly and painfully.
He jolted upright. He looked around the darkness of his room. Nothing to see but the slight glimmer of light from under the door. His heart was pounding and he was covered in sweat. He wasn't sure what had woken him—a bad dream or ... or something else.

He took in some deep breaths of the cool air through his nostrils and out through his mouth, like he'd learned from some guided meditation video a few years back. Four seconds in, hold for seven seconds, release for eight, repeat—

A thumping noise.

It came somewhere from his left. Somewhere outside his room and down the corridor. And that scared him a little. This place was usually so quiet. Every now and then, you'd hear the sound of gunfire as whoever was on night duty shot down oncoming zombies before they became a problem.

But this thumping noise inside the hangar. It was different. It was unsettling.

He climbed to the edge of his bed—a tall metal desk with a thin sleeping bag on top—and he listened. The arrival of Holly had lifted his guard. She appeared honest. Her story seemed genuine. But there was something about the situation—not necessarily about Holly—that Hayden found difficult to trust.

In the same way, he found everyone and everything difficult to trust these days.

He wiped his sleepy, heavy eyes and yawned. He had no idea what time it was, and he had no clue whether he'd drifted off for a few minutes or several hours. All he knew was that it was dark, and yesterday had taken its toll. Losing Tim. The arrival of Holly. Her talk of being bitten and some extraction point in Holyhead. It was a lot to take on board, a lot to understand.

They had to talk. All of them. They had to discuss the next step. Just not now. Not while this place was still standing. Leaving was too risky. They'd left the bunker and look at the losses they'd suffered since then.

No. They couldn't trust anyone. They couldn't—

Another thumping sound, again from the left.

Hayden stopped rubbing his eyes and stayed perfectly still. He listened to the silent hum of the corridor. That thump was definitely not the sound of a gunshot. It was the sound of someone hitting a wall.

Hard.

He reached under his bedsheets, pulled out the seven-inch knife, and he climbed down from his bed and walked over to his door.

He opened his door as quietly as he could. If someone was awake and doing something they shouldn't be doing, Hayden didn't want them to know he was coming. He looked down the left of the corridor. Dim light flickered from the halogens lining the walkway. The silver doors which made up Sarah, Martha, Gary, Matt and Karen's, and now Holly's rooms were all shut.

But there was a thumping sound coming from one of them.

One of them on the left.

Hayden crept slowly down the corridor, knife in hand. He felt the cold tiles seeping through the hardened skin of his feet. He thought about Holly, about how they'd left her locked inside that third door on the left all on her own. It was windowless, and there was no way she could break the lock.

Unless that's what the banging was. Someone trying to break the lock.

Hayden had flashes of her being a part of the Riversford group who had fled this place.

Visions of her breaking out of her room.

Stabbing Martha and Amy to death in the night.

He felt his heartbeat racing as he stepped closer to Holly's door. His mouth was dry. The sound of his own feet patting on the floor made him look forwards, backwards, convinced someone else was out here in the darkness, watching, waiting.

He stood outside Holly's door. Looked at the rust around the circular handle. He watched the door. Watched and waited for it to thump forward.

He lifted his knife. Readied himself. If she was a threat, he had to be willing to neutralise the threat. There was no room for blind sentimentality anymore, only for action.

He held his breath.

Listened to the sound of the wind whistling under the main corridor door.

Waited for—

A thump. A bang. A rattle.

Only it wasn't from Holly's door.

Hayden looked to the right of Holly's room. He looked at the door that was six, seven feet away. It couldn't be. Why would that be banging? Why would they be ...

And then he saw it for real.

The door to Matt and Karen's room shaking on its hinges.

Thump.

Thump.

Thump.

Hayden lowered his knife a little, but not out of ease. If anything, it made him feel more *un*easy that it was Matt and Karen's door that was shaking. Because why would it be? They were grieving, yes. And they had their son in there with them, which was completely wrong, but ...

Unless ...

Hayden's gut hardened. He felt every muscle in his body tighten up.

Tim hadn't been bitten. They'd checked him for bites.

A thump at the door.

And then another.

But what if?

Hayden wiped his nose and blinked heavily. He lifted his knife again and approached the door to Matt and Karen's room. A shiver enveloped him, and it only dawned on him then that all he was wearing was his black and white striped boxer shorts. He stepped further across the cold tiles, closer to the door, closer and closer until he was right in front of it.

He stood there in the silence and waited for another thump.

Waited and waited.

Nothing.

He looked to his left. All the other bedroom doors were closed. He felt that sudden sense of uncanny which so often slipped into his dreams. This was a dream. It had to be a dream. It had to be.

But then he looked at his hands and the palms weren't moving and morphing like they did in dreams, his visual cue to drift into *Inception*-like lucidity.

So he turned back to the door. Stood outside it a little longer. Listened.

"M ... Matt? Karen?"

His voice sounded so loud in this corridor. It echoed off the metallic walls. Echoed so loudly that surely everyone had to hear him.

Unless everyone was dead.

No. He couldn't think like that. He couldn't even contemplate it.

"Matt?" he said again, a little louder this time. "Karen? I-I heard banging. Are you ..."

And then he saw the handle turn.

He lowered the knife, too, felt relief trickle through him. They were just grieving. Matt was just banging the door in the agony of his loss, the frustration. They were just ...

And then he saw Matt staring at him with bloodshot eyes, and the next thing Hayden knew he was on the floor, and Matt was on top of him.

Hayden struggled with Matt. Matt was gasping at him, bloody saliva dripping down from the corners of his mouth.

"Some-someone!" Hayden shouted. He tried to swing at Matt with the knife but then he felt something grab his right arm—and that something was Karen.

He saw Matt's teeth get closer to him, his mouth wide and his breath ghastly. He saw him closing in and he had to move, he had to act.

So he pulled his head back and cracked his forehead into Matt's as hard as he could.

He heard a mini-explosion in his head. He thought for a second he actually felt his brain shake.

Matt fell back a few inches, blood drooling from his broken nose, covering his pale lips.

And then Karen, flesh and skin dangling from her teeth, went to wrap her mouth around Hayden's arm.

Hayden grabbed the knife with his left hand while Matt still struggled to bite his neck. He stuck the knife in the way of Karen's mouth. She bit down on the blade so hard that her teeth cracked, the roof of her mouth split, blood spurted out.

Hayden tried to pull the knife away but it was stuck. It was wedged.

Matt pushed Hayden's arm down.

Opened his mouth.

Went into Hayden's neck, to his jugular, readied for the kill.

And then Hayden heard a blast and he felt blood spill over him.

And then another blast and his knife came free from Karen's mouth.

Hayden pulled himself away. His cold, half-naked body was drenched in blood. He looked to his left, saw Sarah standing there holding a pistol and pointing it at Hayden. Her face was pale. "You … are you …"

"I'm-I'm okay," Hayden said, standing up, although that was a complete lie. He was anything but okay. He was shaken up. Trying to understand how this had happened. "I-I think Tim's bit. I think he must've—must've been bit and …"

He lifted his knife and walked over to Matt and Karen's door. He had to be ready for Tim. He had to be willing to put him down. It was the right thing to do. The peaceful, kind thing to do. Tim must've been bitten. He had to have been bitten. And then he'd woken and bitten his mum and his dad and …

Hayden stopped at the door.

He tried to understand what was in front of him, but all he felt was nausea welling up inside, nausea and adrenaline and fear.

Tim was on the floor. He was exactly where he was when Hayden had last been in this room. He was still staring up into nothingness with those bloodshot, dead eyes. There wasn't a sign of blood on his mouth aside from that which had trickled down his face earlier. His body looked clean. Yellowing, but clean.

"Is he there?" Sarah asked. "Is he … shit."

She stood beside Hayden and she must've seen it too. She must've, because it's the only way anyone could ever be knocked into silence after what they'd just witnessed, what they'd just experienced.

"What—what does it mean?" Sarah asked.

Hayden swallowed a sickly tasting lump in his throat and stared at the blood-smeared letters on the floor in front of him. "I don't know. But I ... I think we need to get out of here."

He wasn't exactly sure how far out of here he meant just yet, but the blood-smeared words in front of Tim's body sent a skin-crawling alarm bell ringing through Hayden's thoughts.

KAREN NOT BIT HES AIRBOURNE TIM AIR—

TEN

The sunrise was cold and unwelcoming.
Hayden stood outside the hangar where they slept. Everyone was outside—Gary, Sarah, Martha, Amy, and Holly. They all stood around in a circle rubbing their cold, goose-pimpled arms. Some of them had clothes wrapped around their mouths. All of them stared, longing and thoughtful, into the flames in front of them. Everyone was quiet. Understanding last night's turn of events at their own pace.

Hayden smelled the fumes from Matt, Karen and Tim's burning bodies and he tightened the scarf around his mouth.

It had been four hours since the discovery of the trio. The discovery of Matt and Karen's undead bodies. And of Tim's body, still dead and cold on the floor.

Since those words written across the floor in blood that Hayden couldn't etch from his mind no matter how hard he tried.

KAREN NOT BIT HES AIRBOURNE TIM AIR—

Hayden had checked Tim's body after reading those words. He'd put gloves on, covered his mouth, and checked every inch of him. Gary had done the same. So too had Sarah, and Martha, and even Holly.

No bites. Not a single wound.

He hadn't died of a bite. He hadn't risen and bitten his mum or dad. He'd passed it on through the air somehow, presumably through Karen considering she too was completely bereft of bite marks.

Hayden imagined the fear and the confusion Matt must've felt when his wife rose and wrapped her teeth around his neck.

He imagined Matt's desperate attempts to scrape a message on the floor in blood in his dying moments.

A warning.

"So what ... what now?"

Martha's voice split the collective silence like a carving knife through hot turkey. Hayden looked at her. Looked at the black scarf covering her mouth. Over her shoulder in the distance, Amy stood. Martha didn't want her little girl anywhere near these bodies. And Hayden knew Newbie wouldn't want that either. Death was very much a part of life now, but it was important to protect a child's innocence. Otherwise, what was the point to anything anymore? If kids couldn't be kids—if even children couldn't see some light at the end of a dark and winding tunnel, then what hope was there for the next generation and the one after that?

It was for that exact same reason that Hayden hadn't told Martha or Amy about knowing Newbie. He wanted to. He wanted to tell them what a brave man he was. But whenever he came close, he saw Newbie's body lying outside that house, leg snapped, blood spurting out of his shoulder.

He felt himself lifting the axe above Newbie's head, wedging it into his neck.

He heard the sound of Newbie's spine cracking and he lost his strength. Because Newbie hadn't died with dignity. He'd been euthanised. Euthanised in a mad few seconds before a crowd of zombies reached Hayden and his sister.

There was no dignity in death. Never had been, never would be. Hayden saw that now.

"We can—we can clear out another of the hangars," Gary said, his voice uncharacteristically raspy. "Somewhere else to stay in case ... well. In case this thing spreads, like."

"We can't stay here," Holly said. "Surely after all that's happened we can't even think about staying here."

"And who made you the authority on what we do around here?" Martha said. Hayden could hear the grief in her voice. "You've been here five minutes and already you're tellin' us what we can and can't do."

"Martha," Sarah said, raising a hand.

"No I won't back down," Martha said. She shook her head. Tears welled in her eyes. "This place, it's—it's ideal. It's good for us. We've got food and water and we've got four walls and a pillow to rest our heads on. It ain't perfect, but it's ... well, it's as safe as we're gonna get. It's home now. I can't take my daughter away into the outside world again. Not again. I can't do that."

"We might not have to be unsafe," Holly said. She scratched at the fresh white bandage on her arm and her dark eyes turned to Hayden.

Hayden felt the light of responsibility fall on him. He hadn't told the rest of the group about Holyhead. Mostly because he hadn't had much of a chance. But he wasn't sure how they'd take it. He knew it would only cause factions and splits within the group, and he'd hardly had a perfect opportunity to speak about it in light of what had happened.

But right now, he knew he had to say something. He knew he had to pitch the idea. Because otherwise, what else did they have?

"I know a place," Holly said, doing his job for him. She looked around at the rest of the group as she spoke, making eye contact with each and every one of them. "When I was with my last group, I heard of an extraction point in Holyhead."

"Where the boats are?" Gary asked.

Holly nodded. "The ferry crossing to Ireland."

Holly told the group what she'd told Hayden the night before. About her reluctance to head that way after being bitten. About her self-defeat, and then about the hope rising as she realised she might be different, she hadn't turned after all.

"I know it's a long shot," Holly said, "and it's hardly my intention to drag you away from a place where you've obviously all got a lot of attachment to. But I guess I'm asking for your help. If I haven't turned, then maybe … maybe there's something in me. Something that can help people. And if this virus is spreading through the air now, maybe I … well, maybe I'm more important than ever."

She looked into Hayden's eyes again when she said these words. And a part deep inside Hayden's mind found himself agreeing with her the more she spoke.

"And how're we s'posed to trust you?" Martha said. "How're we s'posed to know this ain't a loada bullshit just to lure us to some bad place like … like this used to be?"

Holly looked Martha right in her eyes. "I'm going to be honest with you. You aren't supposed to trust me. Because it's dangerous to trust anyone—"

"Well that's that settled," Martha said. She turned and started to walk back to Amy, who lingered a few metres away.

"But I've been bitten and I haven't turned and the way I see it, there's no reason for me to lie about that. And I need your help. I can't make it on my own. But if I have to try, I'll try. I'm not forcing any of you to come with me. I wish I could, but I can't. I'm just trying to survive here. Survive and help."

Sarah shook her head. "I dunno if—"

"I think Holly's right," Hayden said.

He wasn't sure where the words came from exactly, but he totally believed them as he spoke them.

Martha stopped and glared at Hayden. "You what?"

"We can stay here and we can risk dying in here. We don't know how this infection or this virus spreads now. What happened with Tim and his parents ... that changed things. And now I'm starting to wonder if there's more to ... more to life than playing house here."

Martha shook her head. "Keeping my daughter safe ain't playing anything."

"I don't trust you, Holly. Like you said, it would be wrong to trust you. And I swear to God I'll tear your guts out and put you through more pain and misery than you can even comprehend if you betray us. Just like I did to the last person who crossed me. And the one before that. So just bear that in mind. Bear it in mind at all times."

Holly lifted her hands. Hayden saw a flicker of fear in her expression. "I don't have any other motive than survival and maybe helping other people out. If I've been bit and not turned, maybe there's more like me. Maybe they're looking for people like me."

"Humble girl, aren't you?" Sarah asked.

Holly ignored that one.

Hayden and the group watched the last of the flames flicker across the charred remains of the three bodies. They didn't speak, not for some time.

"I don't feel safe here anymore," Hayden said. "And I ... I've had a glimpse of what might be on the other side. We all have. So we need to try something. We stay here and risk tearing each other apart or we go out there and—"

"Risk being torn apart," Martha said.

"It's a risk I'm willing to take if it means saving lives," Hayden said. "So ... so who's with me?"

Hayden looked at Sarah, Gary and then at Martha and Amy. They were still. All of them were still. And Hayden began to feel foolish—like he'd made a massive mistake—like Holly was reeling him in with those powerful eyes and ...

"S'pose I'm with you."

Gary stepped forward. He half-smiled at Hayden, then nodded at Holly.

Hayden felt a slight wave of relief. "That makes three of us. Does—"

"Oh what the hell?" Sarah said. She stepped forward and joined Hayden, Holly and Gary in this messed-up circle of trust. "We're gonna fucking rot at some point anyway. Might as well rot trying to do something good."

She stepped up to Holly. Squared right up to her.

"But Hayden's wrong when he says he'll put you through more pain than you can imagine if you step out of line, missy." She edged even closer, leaned over Holly. "Just wait 'til I get started with you."

She moved away, and Holly had a look on her face like a new kid in a playground desperate to make friends with a group of thugs.

Hayden looked beyond the smoke at Martha and Amy. They stood in the distance, watched the others, both of them completely still.

"Don't make me beg you to come with us," Hayden said. "Please."

Martha shook her head and tightened her grip around Amy. "My duty as a mum's to look out for my little girl in the way I see's fit. And I don't see this journey of yours as fit. So I'm sorry but you're on your own."

She nodded at Hayden, at the rest of the group, and then she turned around and walked towards one of the hangars.

Amy looked back at Hayden as she walked away with her mum. And right then, Hayden wanted to tell her everything. Everything about Newbie, about how brave her dad was. About how hard he'd fought to get to her. About how much he loved her.

But then Amy turned around and the moment was gone, again.

Gone for good.

"Better get a roadmap then," Gary said. "Looks like we're goin' on a journey."

ELEVEN

When Hayden climbed over the fences of Riversford, he felt a part inside of him fade away to ashes.

As he walked across the main road and into the fields opposite Riversford, towards the trees, he felt a distinct urge to turn back. Sarah, Gary and Holly were with him, but Martha and Amy were staying behind. Nothing Hayden could say to Martha would possibly tempt her to leave.

Except he had a feeling there would've been something he could've said. He could've told Martha how much hope Newbie had for his daughter. How optimistic he was about a brighter future, and how he fought to the very end.

But that moment had gone now. That opportunity had passed. Martha and Amy were staying behind. Staying behind in the very place that Tim had died and Karen had turned, all without being bitten.

Staying in the clutches of the unknown.

And yet, there was a bigger sense of security surrounding Riversford than there were the grounds outside.

"Pretty depressing when you think about it," Sarah said.

Hayden looked to his left at her. She was walking through the fields beside him, her brown walking boots squelching through the muddy grass that the sun shone down on. Winter was heading into its final act, which meant that the frosty grass that greeted them every morning was defrosting more readily. As the sun rose a little earlier every day, so too did the optimism, the hope.

And yet Hayden knew he had no idea what he was optimistic about, what he was hoping for.

"What is?" he asked.

Sarah turned around and looked back at Riversford. Studied it with her radiant blue eyes. Her dark brown winter coat was unzipped halfway, revealing a dirty white shirt underneath. Her blue jeans were splattered with mud and something that looked like blood. "That we were happy back there. Content back there."

Hayden turned and looked back at Riversford. He saw the faint outlines of the metal hangars, saw the leafless trees scattered around the grounds beyond the makeshift walls. "It served its purpose. Kept us safe. Wasn't so bad."

"But to think it was the end goal for us. Just … just some industrial tip with decent walls around it and a stinky damp room to sleep in at night. To … to think we were content there. That we were happy that we had that place. It's like back at the bunker. Is this all we're living for now? Stopgaps on the road? One junkyard after another?"

Hayden thought about Amy and Martha being stuck back in Riversford. He tried to picture them firing shots at the zombies when they surrounded the fences or repairing the makeshift walls whenever a brick fell out of place. He thought of their solitude. Just the two of them, and maybe one day just one of them. And then he felt an incredible guilt. He'd made a silent promise to Newbie that he'd find his daughter and look after her. And yet here he was, marching away at the first opportunity without even attempting to win Martha and Amy over.

"Do you think they'll be alright?"

Hayden looked ahead and saw Gary staring back at Riversford

too. He could see the genuine look of concern on his bearded face. Beside him to the right, Holly, who was dressed in a black coat and black trousers way too big for her. She glanced back at Riversford with casual interest. But there was no connection in her look. No real sentimentality. And why would there be? All Riversford was to her was a stopgap. A temporary shelter where she'd finally found company to help her get to Holyhead.

Holyhead. Just thinking about it made Hayden's stomach turn.

"They made their choice," Sarah said, turning away from Riversford and carrying on walking. "We gave them the option to leave that place and Martha made the right call for her and her daughter."

"Just dunno how you can say that's the right call," Gary said. His cheeks were reddening. He fumbled with the sleeves of his grey Mackintosh.

"Not to us, maybe," Sarah said. She put a hand on Gary's arm. "But Martha has a daughter to think about. And Holyhead's a long journey to take on a ... well, it's a long journey to take."

Hayden could sense the apprehension in Sarah's voice. The doubt about this journey. "If there's someone there waiting for us in Holyhead, we can tell them about this place. We—we just need to know for sure. We need to ... to check it out. And then we can go back for Martha and Amy. Help them."

Sarah, Gary and Holly all looked at Hayden with apprehension like he was a crazy person talking crap.

And Hayden understood exactly why. It's because he *was* talking crap. There was no going back for Martha or Amy. Who in their right minds would take a risk like that?

They'd made their decision. They were gone.

And in this world, gone really was gone.

"Come on," Holly said, leading the group. "It'd be nice to be out of the open and in those trees over there sometime soon. Then we can figure out which way we're actually supposed to be heading."

Hayden looked back at Riversford. He looked back at it and he remembered the hope he'd felt when he first laid eyes on it. Or was he misremembering? Had he felt hope or had he felt apprehension right from the off?

Had he felt the same way about Riversford as he now felt about Holyhead?

"Hayden?" Sarah said.

Hayden swallowed a lump in his throat. He thought about Clarice. Thought about her kneeling on the ground while Ally sliced her head off her neck. He thought about Newbie—Newbie's drive and determination to reach his daughter, the hope in his face when he found that note in Martha's old house.

And then he thought about Tim. Tim, dead on the ground for no apparent reason. And then Karen, turned without the first sign of a bite wound.

He cleared his throat.

Felt his face getting a little clammy.

He took a deep breath of the fresh late winter air and he walked.

TWELVE

"How long did you say this is gonna take again?"

Hayden traipsed through the grass. His legs had lost their strength, and the rucksack of weapons and supplies over his shoulder made his body feel like it was going to cave in. Cold sweat stung his lips, and the smell of rot completely engulfed them in this barren woodland.

But that emptiness was also a problem. The complete silence was a problem.

The smell of rot accompanied by ... nothingness. There was something deeply unsettling about it.

"Warrington to Holyhead used to take us a good two hours in the van," Gary said. "And that was goin' the easy route. Right down the motorway. Even with a car, it ain't gonna be possible for us to go down the—"

"How long?" Sarah asked.

Gary moved his fingers through his short hair. "Forty hours. Or so. Two solid days walk without any rest. Talkin'... a week if we bear in mind sleep and—"

"A weck," Sarah said. She shook her head. Hayden could see

the bloodshot tiredness in her eyes. "Knackered after a fucking *hour* and now we're talking about walking a week."

She glared at Holly, but Holly didn't see it. Hayden understood it though. He'd been glaring at Holly this entire journey so far. Not with hatred, not with resentment or anything like that. But with curiosity. Genuine curiosity.

What did she have to gain?

What did she have to lose?

What did they really even know about Holly?

"This transmission," Hayden said, catching up with Holly.

"The one on Harry's phone?"

"You say you heard it?"

Holly nodded. "I saw the words on the screen. Saw all the stuff about an extraction point. There were others, too. Holyhead, Devon, Dover. Figured Holyhead was less of a strain on the—"

"What happened to the people you were with before us?"

Holly stumbled a little. She tried to disguise it as misplacing her footsteps, but Hayden saw it. He saw the question catch her off guard. And he didn't like the surprise on her face. "I told you. Zombies attacked and—"

"You ran off into the woods and found a little cabin to stay in before conveniently dropping by at Riversford a few days after being bitten. I got that part. I still just don't get why."

"And by the sounds of things you never will," Holly said. She turned and looked at Gary and Sarah. "I know how this looks. I know for whatever reason you don't want to trust me. And that's cool. I can handle that. I can live with that. But I know what I saw. I know what happened to me and I know what I saw on that website."

"You said earlier it was a transmission."

"Transmission, website, whatever," Holly said. "Look, I'm not bullshitting you, man. I don't expect you to believe that. But you're out here with me now. We're all out here and we're all heading to Holyhead. So whatever beef you have with me, we all want the same thing here. We're all pulling in the same direction. So can we please just… just not bite each other's balls off about this entire situation? Can we just save some of our energy, maybe?"

Hayden never liked being spoken down to. But he was kind of relieved by Holly's semi-outburst. "Well done," he said. "That's the most honest thing I've heard you say since I first met you."

She didn't have anything clever to say back to that.

They kept on walking through the trees, over the crispy fallen leaves and branches. The woods didn't seem to be getting any thinner. They were heading west, according to Gary. And right now, Hayden was just taking Gary by his word. But he wasn't too sure even Gary knew where he was heading. They could be looping around in these woods, heading anywhere.

"I guess this would be the part of a cheesy bullshit movie where we all talk about our sins before the end times and how fucking damaged we all are," Sarah said.

Holly smiled. "Funny how the worst of clichés are often clichés for a reason."

"Go on then," Sarah said. "What's your story?"

"Oh, not a lot to tell really. Nothing interesting anyway. No partner. No kids. No parents. No siblings."

"On point about the sob story part," Gary said.

"I don't think we mentioned a thing about sob stories," Sarah said.

Gary shrugged. "Musta been getting the clichés mixed up with the reality."

Hayden couldn't tell whether he was being intentionally witty or not.

"What happened to your folks?" Hayden asked.

Holly cleared her throat. "Oh, I er, I lost them after my sister died."

The final words made the muscles in Hayden's body tighten up. "You … How old was your—"

"Eighteen," Holly said. "Anyway, like you say. Nobody wants a sob story. Pass us the water?"

Hayden reached into his rucksack with his shaking hand and he passed out some bottled water. When Holly turned around, she didn't look at him directly, and it was right at that moment that Hayden saw the glimmer of tears building up in her eyes.

"I'm sorry. About your sister. I ... I lost my sister. So I ... I know. How it feels."

She looked up, this time. Looked at Hayden with a look that said so much more than anything anyone had said to him since Clarice had been killed. It was a look of sheer empathy; not of sympathy but of an understanding that transcended words.

He looked back at her in this momentary stasis and he didn't snap out of his trance until he heard the gasps up ahead.

"Wait."

Gary held up his hand. The group stopped walking in an instant, like they'd just run out of batteries. Hayden could hear the gasps up ahead and he could smell the intensifying decay, but he couldn't see anything. Couldn't see anything drifting through the branches, couldn't see anything clawing its way through the trees, reaching their rotten hands out to ...

"There," Sarah said.

It took Hayden a few seconds to realise where Sarah was pointing.

On the ground up ahead, there was a zombie. Its balding middle-aged head was intact, but its chest had been torn to pieces. Inside it, the bloodied remains of a heart punctured by cracked ribs, organs and entrails spilling out onto the bed of the woods.

Its legs and arms had been torn away.

And the worst part about it?

It wasn't the only one.

"Shit," Gary said. "The fuck happened here?"

Hayden looked at the line of zombies splayed out in front of him. They'd been torn to pieces. Torn except for their pitiful heads, mouths snapping away in search of a stray ankle or a flailing arm. Flies feasted and laid maggots on their exposed insides, and the zombies just didn't react, didn't care, just like they didn't react or care about anything.

"Who ... who could do this?" Holly asked. Hayden heard the genuine wonder, the clear amazement in her voice.

Sarah pulled the steel crowbar from her belt and crouched over one of the gasping heads. "I think the question should be *what* could do this," she said.

She slammed the crowbar across one of the fallen zombie's necks. The neck cracked, the zombie went silent.

But the rest of the zombies kept on singing their ghastly song, echoing through the woods' perfect silence.

Hayden looked around at the trees. He thought he saw shimmers of movement in the light, twitching of silhouettes.

And then he looked back at the butchered zombie remains and joined the rest of the group in finishing them off.

He couldn't shake the feeling that he was being watched.

Watched by *something*.

THIRTEEN

After two more hours of walking, Hayden fell to his knees.

Branches snapped underneath him. The dampness of the woodland floor seeped through his jeans onto his legs. No matter how much water he'd drank—and he *was* trying to ration—his throat was dry, and his stomach was calling out with hunger.

And they weren't even a day into their journey.

Gary put a hand on his shoulder. "We'll find some place safer to rest for the night, mate."

Hayden shook his head. "I'm ... I'm starting to think—"

"We can't turn back," Gary said. "Not now. We've come too far. And I ain't mad keen on goin' back to Riversford and gettin' the apocalyptic sniffles anyway. So we push on."

Hayden took some deep breaths into his stomach. A stitch crippled the right side of his body. They could do this. *He* could do this. He could push on through this hurdle and they could reach Holyhead, all of them, together.

He told himself he could do it, he could make it. But the belief wasn't there. It was minuscule. Combated by the pain crippling his exhausted body.

Sarah walked over and put her hand on Hayden's left shoulder. "Gary's right. Don't like saying that too much, but he's right. You need to get up. Isn't safe in here. I'm all for stopping for a rest but not in the middle of this place. Gives me the creeps."

Hayden looked around at the trees, the fallen leaves, the occasional splattering of blood from God-knows-what and God-knows-when. It was the feeling of unease that was getting to him, too. It was like there was no calm moment in this woods because something was constantly watching. And yet that notion was absurd. They'd been lucky. They hadn't encountered a horde of zombies or even a few strays for that matter. Except for the butchered zombies a few miles back, their journey through the woods had been unproblematic.

But that in itself was the problem.

There was no such thing as unproblematic in this world.

Hayden pulled himself up. His legs felt even worse for taking a few seconds of rest. And worse than that, they were damp, so they were cold too. Damp, cold legs for a one week trip. Shit—the chilly confines of Riversford seemed practically five-star next to this.

They moved further through the woods. Sarah led the way sipping at her water, Holly trailing just behind her. Gary and Hayden walked side by side.

"Be straight with me," Hayden said. "D'you actually know where we're going here?"

Gary glared at Hayden. "You doubting me?"

"Yes. To be honest, I am."

Gary shook his head. "Used to drive past these woods all the time on the way down the M56. Always thought they'd be a decent place for a criminal to hang out if their world went to shit or summat."

"Right about that," Hayden said. More rustling to his right. More silhouettes.

Just illusions. Just in your mind ...

"Now you be straight with me," Gary said. "Whaddyou think of her?"

Hayden knew who Gary was talking about right away, but that didn't stop him buying time by asking. "Holly?"

Gary nodded. Hayden hoped he'd reveal a tidbit of what was going through his head, but this answer was on Hayden.

"I want to trust her," Hayden said, lifting his foot over an icy puddle. It was icier the further they got into the woods, the ground sheltered from the sun. "I mean I feel like I should trust her. She seems ... honest. Right?"

Gary just nodded. He didn't say anything, he just nodded.

"You thinking differently?"

"Just think we should keep an eye on her. Just in case. Y'know?"

He looked right at Hayden and Hayden saw the apprehension in his face.

Hayden nodded. "Just in case," he said. "I know what you—"

And then he felt something grasp hold of his right ankle and he fell to the ground.

At first, Hayden thought he'd just slipped on ice.

But then he heard the grunt and heard the cracking sound and he knew they had company.

Sarah and Holly swung around. "Fuck!"

Hayden turned onto his back and kicked at the zombie. It had frozen to the ground completely, its hand now free of its icy shackles. Dark hair stuck to its white cheeks and frost covered a gaping wound on the side of its neck.

Hayden tried to wriggle away but the zombie pushed its teeth up to Hayden's shin and tried to clamp its jaw, frozen open in the ice. He felt its grip getting tighter, heard the ice on its jaw cracking, readied for the searing pain of contact.

Then there was an ear-splitting crack and the zombie went still.

Hayden pulled his ankle free from the tight clutches of the

zombie. He wiped his shivering hands on his coat, backed away, nearly slipping on another sheet of ice in the process.

Over the zombie, Holly stood, a bloodied metal baseball bat in hand.

"You okay?" she asked.

Hayden studied her for a moment and then he nodded. "Yeah. I ... Thanks. I just—"

Another splitting sound from inside the woods.

And then another.

And another.

Then, gasping.

Hayden looked around at the half-frozen zombies dragging their partly thawed bodies from the ground. He reached into his rucksack, pulled out a wrench and a gun, and then he backed up to Gary, Sarah and Holly.

"What—what do we do?" Hayden asked.

The zombies rose from behind them, clambered free of the ice and stumbled in the group's direction.

"We run," Gary said.

FOURTEEN

"We only use the guns if we have to," Hayden shouted.

"I'd say this fucking qualifies as 'have to'," Sarah said.

The group of four sprinted as fast as they could through the trees. The ground switched between icy and thawed as the sun peeked in through cracks in these evergreen trees. Hayden tried to keep his balance. He couldn't slip. Couldn't fall. Not now.

Behind, the guttural groans of the zombies grew ever closer.

"Which way?" Hayden shouted.

"Any way!" Gary said. "Ain't sure directions matter too much right now."

Hayden didn't like that, but shit—he was hardly in a position to argue. So he kept on running. Felt the loose branches of trees scrape against his face, felt his knees tensing up with every awkward step, a stitch spreading through his stomach and threatening to floor him.

"An opening!" Holly said. "Up ahead!"

Hayden didn't have time to scrutinise Holly's words. He told himself not to peek over his shoulder but doing so just prompted him to look.

A dozen of them. At least.

Not a smidgen of frostiness about the way they were moving. Not now.

And then he stumbled forward.

Felt himself floating through the air, like he was moving in slow motion.

And just as quickly as he'd slipped, Hayden found his footing again, kept on running like it was all just part of the plan.

"Which fucking opening are you on about?" Sarah shouted, not giving a shit about how her voice might attract the undead—and with reason. They were attracted as it damned well was.

"I ... I dunno," Holly said. "I swore I saw—"

A half-dozen strong group of zombies staggered from behind the trees up ahead.

"Shit!" Sarah shouted. She stopped running and Holly crashed into her, Gary just about slowing his run before he could fly into them too, Hayden already stationary.

He looked around. Looked behind at the zombies as they marched closer. Some of them were still frozen at the teeth, and Hayden couldn't shake the image of ice-cold fangs slicing through his skin and feasting on his insides. Up ahead, more zombies approached. To the left and to the right, the trees were thicker and it was impossible to see what was hiding beyond those natural walls.

"Need to make a decision right about now," Gary said. "Left or right, guys."

"Fuck it." Hayden lifted his pistol and pointed it at the crowd of zombies heading from behind.

"No!" Sarah said. She knocked the gun down. Stared at Hayden with bloodshot eyes. "We don't absolutely need to. Not yet. We need to move."

Hayden looked at the frosty zombies stepping towards him and right there and then he felt a deep, unavoidable anger and frustration. He knew it was irrational, like being angry at the customer service adviser at a call centre when the real problem was management. But he couldn't help it. He wanted to punish these beasts for the disruption they'd caused to this world. He wanted to punish *anybody* for the disruption to this world.

But not right now.

Right now, he had to move.

Had to get the hell out of here.

He ran to his right into the thicker mass of tree trunks and branches. Darkness seemed to descend on the group as they disappeared into the unknown, the zombies' cries a constant reminder that they were hot on their heels.

They ran. Ran over icy patches and ran over snapped logs and ran over the remains of squirrels and rats, gutted and splayed out all over the bed of the woodland. And as they ran, as the natural taste of the trees covered Hayden's lips and encapsulated his senses, he realised how frigging unfair it was for the human race to go and wreak so much havoc on mother nature. Unintentional havoc, sure, but havoc nonetheless. Havoc that wouldn't even be a conscious idea if it weren't for the presence of humans.

Humans. "They just screw things up," his granddad used to say.

And Hayden hadn't understood what he meant as a kid. He saw the positives to humanity. Technological advances, medical care. Missions into space and democracy-spreading wars.

But right now, he agreed with his old granddad. Humans really did just screw things up, whether they had a conscious hand in it or not.

"Argh!"

The scream snapped Hayden out of his terrified senses.

He looked for Sarah and Holly. But no—they were still on

their feet, running along into the mass of trees, on the brink of disappearing into a nothingness beyond.

On the floor to Hayden's right, Gary lay.

Gary clenched hold of his foot. Blood spilled out of the bottom of his black walking boot. The teeth of a sharp metal fox trap had pierced through the rubber and the leather.

His foot was bloodied and mangled inside it.

Gary screamed. His face was completely pale. He clutched his ankle and stared at his injured foot in disbelief.

"You—you need to get up," Hayden said. He heard the gasps getting closer. Saw the branches behind shaking.

"I—I can't, mate. My foot. Fuck. My fucking foot. My fucking —arghhh!"

Hayden cringed when Gary screamed. And it was a cringe that didn't *feel* right because he knew he was cringing more for his own safety than with Gary's pain.

But he had to make a decision right now. He had to do something.

He looked up. Sarah and Holly getting further away. He was losing sight of them. Fast.

Gary screamed.

Behind, the branches swayed. Gasps got louder. Hungrier. Closer.

Gary screamed.

Hayden crouched beside Gary. "You—you need to be quiet. You need to be quiet or—"

"My foot my fucking foot my—argh!"

Hayden heard the rustling of the branches and the gasps and the cries all as one. He moved his hands towards the rusty, blood-soaked trap. "You need to keep still. We don't have much—"

"Please make it stop. Please make it stop." Tears rolled down Gary's cheeks as he clutched his ankle, stared up at the moving mass of the trees behind, awaiting his fate.

Hayden's heart raced. He'd lost sight of Sarah and Holly completely. Soon it would be just him and Gary. And then Gary would bleed out and it would be just him. Just Hayden, all alone in a deathly woods in the middle of nowhere.

Exhausted. Trapped.

No.

He wrapped his hands around the teeth of the trap and tried to pry it open.

It didn't budge.

Gary roared with pain.

Gary's blood covered Hayden's fingers. And right there, holding Gary's ankle upright, he understood. He understood what this was. He understood the decision he had to make. A cruel decision. An impossible decision. A decision that shouldn't even be in his hands.

But the necessary decision.

"Keep as still as you can," Hayden said. He dropped the rucksack and reached into it with his quivering fingers. In the corner of his eye, he saw the zombies approaching.

"What—what—"

Hayden swung the mallet into the side of Gary's head.

"I'm sorry, Gary," he said. "I'm ... I'm so sorry."

And then he laid down a sharp handsaw at Gary's unconscious side and he stood up and ran.

He ran away from the gasps and the cries of the zombies.

He ran through the branches, onwards and onwards in the trickling glow of the late winter sun.

He ran like someone was controlling him. Someone playing a sandbox video game with multiple routes of good and evil to choose from.

He was never the evil. Ever.

Until now.

No!

He'd done what was right for Gary.

What was kindest.

There was no hope for him.

Nothing.

He ran and ran through the trees and he felt a warm tear roll down his cheek as Gary's blood crusted in his palms.

FIFTEEN

Hayden sprinted through the woods as fast as his wrecked body would allow him.

His feet ached with pain. Every tree he ran past blended into one. Sometimes, he thought he heard a voice—the voice of Sarah or Holly up ahead—but when he emerged from the trees, all he saw was more twigs, more branches, thick, constant, endless.

It was the middle of the day but a darkness hung over Hayden. The darkness of his actions; of what he'd done. He didn't want to admit it. He didn't want to face up to it. But he had to.

He'd knocked Gary out. Left him behind to be feasted on by the oncoming mass of zombies. Left a blade beside him, just in case he woke up and needed to take a stand against the zombies.

Or to make his own decision about the next step.

Hayden felt tears dripping down his chapped, scratched face as he kept on running. Sickness welled at the back of his throat, the smells of death refusing to leave his senses. He'd done the only thing he could for Gary. The only thing that seemed right at that moment in time. Because he was trapped. His foot was wedged in a trap and there was no way out for him, no escape.

He'd done what he had to do. And that was wrong. So, so wrong.

And now he was lost. Lost, alone, in the middle of the woods. Only death awaited him. He knew that now. Accepted it. And in a way, he knew he deserved it for what he'd done. Because there was no bright light at the end of the tunnel in the form of Holyhead. There was no turning back to Riversford for anything other than more death, more destruction.

There was just endless nothing. Endless death.

He slowed down and leaned against the cracked bark of a tree. He panted. Felt a stitch rippling through his stomach and crippling his body. Behind, he couldn't hear the zombies approaching anymore. But he knew they were there. He knew, somewhere behind him, they were there. Because they always were. Everywhere he looked, everywhere he turned, always watching, waiting ...

He hadn't heard Gary scream or cry out. Part of him wasn't sure how to feel about that. On one hand, he was relieved. He didn't want Gary to suffer any pain. He wanted Gary to stay quiet in hope that the zombies wouldn't bite him ... but that was a long shot, he knew.

So the next best thing was that Gary didn't wake up from his unconsciousness. That he stayed trapped in the clutches of sleep, the throes of darkness.

He didn't want Gary to wake up knowing he'd been betrayed.

Hayden's heart pounded.

What have you done?

What have you become?

He crouched down and leaned back against the tree. Tears rolled down his cheeks like falling rain, uncontrollable and unstoppable. He saw flashes of the last few weeks in his mind. Of his parents—of what he'd had to do to them. And then of Newbie, Clarice, of Matt, Karen, and little Tim, and now of Gary.

And then he remembered Ally. Remembered Callum and the

evil that enshrouded him. The things those two—and many others—had done to all those poor women, those poor children.

But Hayden had left a man to die. He'd decided the fate of a friend. He'd signed Gary's death warrant. Who was he to do that?

His body started to shake. He dug his head between his knees, rocked back and forth in the cold darkness. He just wanted out of this. Out of all this. Because he couldn't trust anyone or anything anymore. And the horrifying part about that truth was that he was right—nobody could trust *anybody*. And Hayden was no exception to that rule either.

There was no good in this world, not anymore. There was only what kept you alive.

He sniffed. Smelled the metal and the rot in the air—the smells that might not even be there—and he wished for a way out of this. It was the most like his old self he'd felt since the day of the fall. He cried freely. Blubbered like a fucking baby. He'd kept his emotions, his fear, his sadness, all of it bottled up inside until now.

Nothing but a self-pitying wreck.

And then he heard footsteps cracking through the twigs on the woodland floor.

He looked through the trees. He couldn't see the source of the sound, not at first. Too many branches. Too many trees packed in closely together. It was like a hall of mirrors. Nature's evil hall of mirrors waiting to catch him out.

Then he saw it.

Saw the torn grey jacket.

The bloodied skull.

He saw the blood pooling out of the sinewy neck and the dirty long fingernails peppered with blood and bits of flesh.

Hayden held his breath and kept still as the zombie approached through the trees. A part of his mind screamed out at him to run. To get the fuck away from here. To hide.

But then another part—a stronger part that had been hiding

away in the back of his mind ever since his older sister killed herself—told him to stay put.

Let it take you.

This can all end, right here.

Mum's dead, Dad's dead, Annabelle's dead and Clarice is dead.

And then he saw his family just like he saw them in his nightmares.

Blood soaking them, head to toe.

Bite marks tearing through the sides of their necks.

Beaming smiles. Bright eyes.

Join us join us join us.

The zombie staggered closer. Hayden's body was frozen. He gritted his teeth. Listened to the skin-crawling groan.

Join us Hayden please join us join us.

Five steps away.

Four.

Three.

Annabelle with a belt around her bruised neck.

Clarice holding her head under her arm.

Smiling.

JOIN US JOIN US JOIN—

And then something crashed into the side of the zombie and it fell to the ground.

Someone.

Sarah pushed the knife into the zombie's neck as it wriggled around on the soily woodland. Her face turned as she wedged the knife in even further, pressed in even harder. All the while, Hayden couldn't get the images of his family out of his mind, couldn't stop them singing and dancing and chanting.

Don't leave us please so close please ...

Putting the pillow over Mum's face.

Pressing down.

Mum who gave birth to him. Raised him up. Did everything for him.

Pressing and pressing until her last breath trickled out of her weakened—

"Come on. Get up. Don't wanna stick around here."

Hayden snapped out of his thoughts like he'd been hit in the face. He looked up. Saw Sarah standing over him holding a hand out.

He took a few steadying breaths. Took Sarah's hand and stepped up. His knees were weak. His entire body felt like it'd been through a metal crusher and straightened out at the other end. He looked around, saw Holly standing with her arms folded. She half-smiled and nodded at Hayden, her brown eyes twinkling in the glimmer of light from above.

"Gary," Sarah said. "He not ... not make it?"

Hayden didn't look at Sarah when she said *his* name. He just stared back into the darkness of the woods. He stared back and he saw infinite secrets—infinite secrets and demons that he'd never tell of, never.

They'd stay trapped away in those woods. Confined to history. They had to.

He breathed in a sharp, deep breath and shook his head.

Sarah sighed.

"Come on then," she said. "After what we found, we're gonna wanna get the hell away from here sometime soon."

Hayden followed Sarah and Holly. His thoughts were still dim and unfocused like a radio improperly tuned. "What did you—what did you find?"

Sarah stopped. Pointed ahead. "This."

SIXTEEN

After three minutes of staring at it, Hayden was still stunned by the dismembered body lying in front of him.

It was a man. "Was" being the operative word here. He had thick dark hair and a skinny face. Hazelnut eyes. Probably an attractive lad back when he was alive. The kind of guy Hayden used to spend a lot of his miserable days wishing he was more like. Someone confident with women. Someone who caught people's eye.

Shit. He'd certainly caught Hayden's eye in his current state.

His face was untouched, and there were no signs of trauma except for his eyes, which bulged bloodshot out of their sockets. The chaos started at his neck. It had been bitten right through to the bone, and like a cooked chicken leg at a buffet, all that remained were little sinewy strings of muscle and tendon.

"What ... what do you think did this?" Holly asked. She stared at the man with her wide, terrified eyes, just as stunned and hypnotised as Hayden, even if this wasn't the first time she'd seen the scene.

Hayden licked his dry lips. He examined the body further. Saw the snapped ribs piercing through the broken skin. Saw the bloody mush where the man's organs once were. Saw the gnawed intestines, which flies buzzed around and laid their eggs.

He saw the man's right leg, torn away from the body and bitten down to the bone just like his neck.

"Whatever it was, I don't wanna meet it anytime soon," Sarah said.

The sounds of the branches scratching together in the wind rustled in the background as Hayden stared at the body. Even in spite of the blood and gore on show, in spite of the hot acid climbing up his throat and threatening to surface, it was the man's eyes he kept turning to. The terrified expression. A look like he knew what was happening to him—like he was facing up to the grim brutality of his own death, helpless, defenceless.

Holly stepped around the side of the man and crouched down by his leg. "What's this?"

"You wanna stay back," Sarah said. "You don't wanna—"

A deafening snap of metal.

Holly squealed and fell back.

Hayden knew what it was before he saw it. He remembered the sound when Gary had fallen over. The sound that came just before his pig-like squeal.

The snapping of a trap.

"Shit," Holly said, her voice shaky. She held her hand away and stared at the trap, which had flipped over beside the man's leg. "Shit."

"This is why you shouldn't go fucking touching things," Sarah said. She went to step towards Holly, then stopped, looked around the ground. A heightened awareness of a new danger. They couldn't be careless. Not with traps around.

They couldn't risk being another Gary.

"What d'you think the traps are for?"

Hayden looked around the grass. He looked beyond the man and at a green metal fence. A hole had been torn through the side of it. The metal curled like something had forced its way through it. Something big.

"Makes sense to catch the undead that way," Sarah said, walking towards the fence. "I guess. Right?"

Hayden heard the uncertainty in her voice and he understood it. He wasn't sure if she was right. There was something going on here. Something had torn the zombies up right back in the woods. Something that someone was laying down traps for.

Something big enough to tear a hole in the fence up ahead.

"We should go," Hayden said. "We ... we don't want to stick around here."

"Amen to that," Sarah said.

The three of them walked up to the fence. Holly climbed through the gap first, and Hayden went to follow.

Sarah put a hand on his chest.

She looked him directly in his eyes with narrowed eyes of her own. Her face was pale and gaunt, but those beaming blue eyes looked as piercing as ever. "What happened back there?"

Hayden swallowed the sickly lump in his throat. He turned back in the direction he'd come from. He kept on expecting to hear Gary's dying screams or see him waddling out of the woods with the trap dangling from his leg.

Hungry.

Undead.

Vacant.

Hayden felt his eyes welling up again and he wanted to tell Sarah. He wanted to tell her the truth. He wanted to spill everything out and he wanted her to help him carry this burden.

But he couldn't. He couldn't risk that.

He wasn't sure anyone trusted him as it was. But they definitely wouldn't trust him if they knew the truth.

"Shit. Guys, look at this!"

Hayden heard the fear in Holly's voice. He turned and saw she was standing at the edge of the trees through the fence. She was smiling, and Hayden realised then it wasn't fear in her voice but excitement.

He climbed through, Sarah following closely behind. "What is it?"

Holly pointed ahead through the thinning trees. Her smile widened some more. "Our way out," she said.

Hayden saw exactly what she was talking about, and his heart did a flip.

There was a white golf buggy on a dirt track opposite them. Blood was splattered over its side, and there was a man in a blue uniform lying beside it with sharp teeth marks in his neck. He stared up at the sky, his eyes glassy and vacant. But he didn't move. He showed no signs of life, or of unlife.

The trio rushed towards the golf caddy.

"Jesus Christ, who the hell even drives one of these things?" Sarah said.

"Doesn't matter," Holly said, half-laughing. "Thank God for Mr Anonymous golf buggy driver."

Hayden reached the golf buggy first. He stepped over the dead body of the man lying beside it. The keys were still in the engine.

He held his breath and climbed across the leather seat, which was also dampened with blood. He reached for the key. Felt tension tingling inside him. This had to work. They needed this to work. It could speed them out of the woods, get them back on track to Holyhead.

"What the fuck you waiting for?" Sarah asked, throwing herself into the golf buggy, Holly closely following.

Hayden touched the edge of the keys.

Please work. Please.

He turned the key, and the golf buggy coughed to life.

"Woohooo!" Sarah said. She lifted a hand and high-fived Holly then ruffled Hayden's hair with her damp palms. "Thank fuck for golf buggy driving nerds. Now where?"

Hayden put the golf buggy into "drive" and pressed his foot

down on the accelerator, the cool breeze brushing against his cheeks as they made their way out of the trees down the bumpy, dusty track. "Anywhere but here," he said.

The three of them left the woods, left the man lying on the side of the dirt track with the deep teeth marks in the side of his neck, left the dismembered man further in the woods.

He lay there in the leaves, dead and still, and a shadow descended over him.

Underneath his collar, *Mike Holliday: Chester Zoo, Animal Feeder* glistened in blood.

SEVENTEEN

Gary Howarth felt a crippling pain tear through his right ankle.

He tried to open his eyes but they were heavy, like the time he'd woken up with conjunctivitis as a kid and couldn't open them for hours. Above him, he could see the faint outline of trees contrasting the grey sky. The right side of his forehead wracked with pain, like he'd been hit. Where the hell was he? And how the hell'd he ended up here?

He closed his eyes again and squeezed them together. Damned hangover, probably. Mary-Anne was always nagging on at him to quit the booze. Well, Mary-Anne, you try delivering six zillion parcels a day and see how you like it. Instead of sitting at home all day sponging off my income on your lazy ass, you try getting up and getting a job instead of flirting with the damned next door neighbour. You try—

"Argh!"

The noise escaped his throat reflexively as the sharp pain wedged further into his right ankle. The fuck? Was he in hospital or something? Some kind of accident? Last thing he remembered, he was behind the wheel. No ... no, wait, he was back at CityFast HQ. Back preparing for a day at work. Back …

The memories came to him in a sudden and stark flash.

The dead, walking.

Callum taking Mary-Anne prisoner and forcing Gary to do his dirty work.

Murder.

Death.

Bloodbath.

And then Hayden …

He remembered Hayden with mixed emotions. Part of him told him this Hayden guy was a good guy. An honest man who had everyone's best interests at heart.

But there was something about Hayden he didn't like for some weird reason just out of his grasp. Some deep sense of inexplicable hate that he couldn't explain, no matter what.

He took in a deep breath of the putrid air and felt himself getting closer and closer to the truth when he felt the pain in his right ankle again.

He looked down at his right ankle and just as quickly as he didn't understand, he understood. He was running away from something. Running away with … that's it. With Hayden, Sarah, that other girl whose name escaped him right now. He was running away and then … and then he'd slipped. No—he'd stepped in *this* thing. This thing wrapped around his ankle.

A sharp animal trap splitting through his trousers.

He saw his own blood and muscle and he felt a cold wave tumble over him. Dizziness filled his head. There was a lotta blood on the ground around him. Lotta blood he'd lost. Amazing he was still alive. Amazing he was …

And then he remembered something else.

Hayden stopped. He tried to help Gary because—because the zombies were coming. Coming through the trees. That's right: the zombies were coming through the trees and Hayden was desperate, trying to help Gary, trying and trying to get him out of this mess.

And then Gary heard Hayden apologising and before he could ask what for he felt something crack against his face and then …

Blackness.

His heart raced. The muscles in his jaw tightened. That was it. Hayden had screwed him over. Clubbed him to fuckin' unconsciousness and left him to die out here. Didn't matter how damned sorry he was or not, he'd screwed him.

He'd pay. He'd fuckin' pay.

Gary lifted his body upright. The muscles in his stomach were weak and sore. Every twitch of his right leg made the pain shoot right through his body, split through his spine and the top of his skull. Cold sweat rolled down his forehead, dripped down his face. He had to get out of this shit-trap. He had to get to Hayden. He had to—

A rustling in the trees to his left.

He looked up. Looked at where the rustling came from. Branches swaying in the breeze. Fallen leaves. Even further back, the black thickness of evergreen trees looming large.

But nothing moving.

He looked back at his ankle and the handsaw by its side caught his eye.

He recognised the saw. One of the weapons from Riversford. Sharp as fuck, good enough to split through any zombie's neck or limb.

Or human's limb …

He reached for the handsaw and lifted it in his quivering hand. An idea formed in his mind. Damned stupid idea, out here in the cold and the middle of nowhere. But an idea nonetheless. A chance of getting out of here.

He pictured pressing the sharp blade of the handsaw to his leg.

Splitting through the top layer of skin.

Slicing through the muscle.

Scraping through the bone ...

"Fuck," Gary said. He lowered the handsaw. Ain't no chance he was choppin' his own leg off anytime soon. Sure, that bloke off *Saw* had survived it enough to spawn six damned sequels, but that was fiction and this was reality.

Chop his leg off and he was done for.

Or ... wait. *127 Hours* with James Franco. He chopped his leg off and he lived long enough to make it out to safety.

Or was it his arm he chopped off?

Was it real?

Did it even matter?

Gary felt his teeth chattering as he lay there in complete silence. Silence, but for the rustling of the trees in the breeze. The singing of the last remaining birds, oblivious to the chaos around them.

He looked up at the sky, saw still in his hand, and he shouted: "Hello!"

Figured he was an idiot right away. Didn't want to attract any zombie attention. But maybe there was someone nearby.

There had to be someone nearby.

He couldn't saw himself out of this.

He had to saw himself out of this ...

He felt tears building up. Felt fear mounting in his chest like a child who'd lost their mummy in the middle of a supermarket. He looked back down at his fucked up ankle. And then he looked at the saw. What other choice did he have? What other damned choice had Hayden left him with?

He sunk his teeth into his lips and he moved the blade over his leg. He tried not to think about what he was about to do. Tried not to think about the repercussions. Cause he was a dead man if he stayed here. He'd bleed out. Or the zombies would get him. Or both. And he couldn't have that. He was a trier. He'd never die without at least trying to do something.

He pressed the blade against his skin and thought about the games of football he used to play in the CityFast yard with his mates on lunch break. The pile-driver shots to the back of the nets, which were marked by the cardigans of his friends—his friends who had fallen, been corrupted, or both.

He swallowed the frog in his throat and pressed down on the leg just above his ankle. He felt the sharpness right away. Felt warm blood trickle down the blade and onto his fingers. He felt the piercing pain of each tooth of the blade stick into his skin, his flesh, and he grit his teeth even further.

He waited. Waited to pull it back and start the slicing. Because once he started, there was no stopping. Once he started, it was all or nothing.

He gritted his teeth.

Pushed the blade down.

Come on. You can do this. You can do this ...

Tensed his upper arm, tightened his fingers.

Three. Two. One ...

And then his biceps went weak and he dropped the blade from his fingers.

He leaned forward and he cried. He cried for the people he'd lost and the shit they'd been through. But mostly he cried for himself. Because he was a decent bloke. Hadn't stolen a parcel in his life. Always smiled at grumpy customers and tried to tame the yappiest of dogs.

What had he done to deserve this?

What had he ...

He heard the rustling again.

He looked at the source of the sound. His heart pounded. He couldn't see properly through the cloudy tears in his eyes. His mind wanted to convince him that there was nothing there. He was okay. He was gonna find a way out of here. Cause it wasn't his turn to die yet. He'd imagined all kinds of ways his life might end, but all of 'em were peacefully in a deathbed aged seventy-something when it was *time* to go.

But when he saw the thing coming towards him, jet black eyes focused on him, he started to doubt those assurances after all.

He shuffled away. Shuffled away even though it sent splitting pain through his ankle. He whimpered. "Go away. P-please. I don't mean no harm. Don't mean no—please!"

He stuck his fingers of his left hand into the soil and tried to yank himself away. He felt the skin and muscle of his right leg splitting as he did, felt warm blood dribble down its side, but still he kept on pulling, just to get away from that ... from that *thing*. That impossible thing.

He felt his bladder give way as the footsteps pounded closer, the grunts and growls edged nearer. His bowels followed soon afterwards. But lying there in his own shit and piss, vomit sneaking up from his stomach, he kept on pulling at the sharp teeth of the trap, scraping his skin and muscle away, hot pain splitting through him, desperate not to die, convinced this wasn't his moment.

When he felt the sharp pain split through the back of his left leg with the force of a million damned animal traps; when he felt the beast rip the muscle away and felt the blood dribble from its satisfied mouth and onto his body, he knew right then that this *was* in fact it. This was the moment he went. This was his swan song.

He started to drift into agonising unconsciousness when the beast came in for another bite of his lower back with its knifelike teeth, and this cycle repeated itself on and on and on for what felt like forever to Gary, who didn't even have it left in him to scream.

And when he thought it was over, when he was convinced it was done, full, satisfied, he lifted his weak head and he saw more movement coming his way.

A lion cub, coming to join the feast.

EIGHTEEN

The winding dirt track was long and spiralled on for miles, and Hayden felt like eyes were watching him every inch of the way.

Invisible eyes peeking through the trees. Rustling movement. Growling.

"Is it just me or is this place completely and utterly ... well, off?" he asked.

Holly sat by Hayden's side, Sarah now manoeuvring the golf buggy. He'd had difficulty steering it. Always had been shit when it came to vehicles. First realised that back at the dodgems at Blackpool Pleasure Beach many a year ago.

She smiled. "It's empty and you're complaining about it seeming 'off'. Trust really isn't your strong point, is it?"

"If you'd seen the things I've seen, it wouldn't be yours either." He diverted his gaze away from Holly. He didn't want her to catch him looking at her with accusation and curiosity. He didn't want her to see the glimmer of truth in his eyes—the truth of what he'd done to Gary. Leaving him behind, unconscious, to die in the way he had.

"He was hardly the most trustful bloke *before* he saw the shit he talks about," Sarah said, steering the vehicle around a sharp curve in the road.

"Oh yeah?" Holly laughed. "How did you guys meet anyway?"

"Hayden here was—"

"That's a story for another time," Hayden interjected. He felt his cheeks heating up at the memory of being stood at the side of his old road. The desperation and the fear inside him as Sarah shouted at him to get into the back of the van. He thought about how hopeless he'd felt, how hopeless he must've looked. It wasn't an image he wanted Holly to see, not right now. "How far d'you think 'til we hit the roads again anyway?"

Sarah took another turn. "Your guess is as good as mine. Tell you what, this place is weird. The fuck's that thing there?"

Hayden looked where she was pointing. Some kind of cabin beside a lake. The lake looked artificial, like it had been dug up recently. Behind it, a tall, sturdy-looking metal fence to keep whatever was on the other side out of here.

"Some kind of new development?" Holly asked.

Hayden thought back to the state of the bodies he'd seen recently. To the hole torn in the side of the fence near where they found the buggy. And of the traps. Why would there be traps in the woods? What was so dangerous that it required capturing?

"I know something happened. Back there. With—with Gary."

The words from the left made Hayden's face turn cold. He looked to his side. Saw Holly with her head down. She was holding her dry hands together, fumbling and scratching at them.

"What ... I don't ..."

"I can see that look on your face," Holly whispered. "I can see that look because I've had that look on my face before, too. You changed when you walked out of those woods. Something on your face. You can tell me. If there's ... if you have a secret, you can tell me."

Hayden's mouth dried out completely. He looked at Sarah, who fast shifted her gaze away like she was pretending not to look. Hayden cleared his throat. He couldn't be the one in the spotlight here. "Stuck in a golf buggy with a woman who claims she's been bitten and hasn't turned, and also claims she knows a safe place in Holyhead. And I'm the one who's being scrutinised?"

"Hey," Holly said. "We had this discussion. We've talked about honesty and trust and—"

Sarah coughed.

"And I'm allowed my reservations, like you said," Hayden said. "I just don't agree with you tearing apart my—"

"I'm not tearing a thing apart. I'm simply—"

Sarah coughed.

"I know what you're trying to—"

And then the golf buggy veered off the dirt track.

When Hayden realised what was happening, it was already too late.

He looked at Sarah as the golf buggy veered towards the trees. She was lying with her head on the steering wheel. Her arms had gone limp and her eyes were closed.

Blood oozed from her nostrils.

Hayden lunged for the steering wheel but before he could reach it, he heard the metal buggy crack and his body flew out of the side of the vehicle.

He crashed into the muddy ground. Tumbled and tumbled on his side, branches scratching his cheeks, the taste of blood building up in his mouth. He tried to stop his roll but it was pointless. He was going too fast. Speeding down the hill towards a stream. If he didn't stop soon, his head would crack on the rocks and it would be over, everything would be over.

He stuck his fingers into the mud. Felt it slip away under his grip. He had no idea where Holly or Sarah were but he could hear movement, feel their eyes on him.

He stuck his fingers into the ground again, shifted all his weight into the earth.

With a finger-snapping jolt, he stopped.

He caught his breath. The sounds of the trees rustling in the wind surrounded him. The taste of blood was strong now. His ears rang like a gun had fired either side of them.

He closed his eyes, squeezed them together, tried to balance himself.

Then he remembered: Sarah.

The look on her face. Blood dripping down from her nose. The cough. And then the unconsciousness.

And then he remembered little Tim. Little Tim, who didn't have a sign of a bite wound on his body, and went on to pass the virus to his mum.

The panic on Sarah's face when she'd first found Tim's body. The blood on her hands.

Matt's words etched in blood: *KAREN NOT BIT HES AIRBOURNE TIM AIR—*

He eased his tender body around in the direction of the rustling, the movement, and he saw it.

A zombie wearing a bloodied blue uniform just like the man who had been butchered back where they'd found the golf buggy.

It was marching in Hayden's direction. Reaching its long, sharp fingers out, the bones peeking through the gnawed-down tips.

Hayden tensed his body. Tried to lift himself up, but his ribs stung, his head ached.

The zombie ran. Ten metres away. Nine metres. Soon, it'd be upon him. He'd be a goner. It'd be over. It'd—

Something shifted in the right of his vision.

It happened in a blur. A dreamlike blur that Hayden couldn't comprehend—and probably never would.

Something jumped out and landed on the zombie.

Something big. Golden.

An animal.

It knocked the zombie to the ground. Hayden heard its neck crunch as the beast's paw pressed into it. He saw the saliva dribble from the corners of the beast's mouth, saw it go in to bite the zombie with its piercing sharp teeth.

And then he saw it turn away. Grunt in dissatisfaction, like Hayden might if he smelled some off milk.

It lifted its head—its huge, gorgeous head—and only then did Hayden truly understand what he was looking at.

It was the undeniable face of a lion. A lion with a beautiful golden mane. Through its fur, Hayden could see its ribs.

The lion looked at Hayden with its big, brown eyes.

Stared at him. Sniffed the air.

"Holy shit." Holly's voice from somewhere behind. "Is that …"

Hayden didn't hear the rest of what Holly had to say.

Blood-laced drool dripped from the hungry lion's mouth.

The beast stepped towards him.

NINETEEN

The last time Hayden stared a lion in the eye was when he was back in high school on a school trip to Knowsley Safari Park. He remembered his coach driving past the crowd of three, four lions, all lying down, all looking back at him. He remembered the fear he felt. The realisation that, if they wanted to, those beasts could wander over to the school coach and butcher everyone inside. Every last one of them.

Except that day, he remembered the tour guide insisting the lions were well fed. That they weren't hungry. And that they were actually rather timid of vehicles.

Today, over a decade later, Hayden wasn't guarded by the protection of a vehicle.

He wasn't trapped behind glass, observing from a distance.

And the lion didn't look well-fed.

He wanted to move away. Wanted to drag himself up the grassy ridge, back towards the dirt track. But as he stared at this lion—saw its ribs poking out of its matted fur, saw blood from the creature dripping down its mane—all he could do was stay put. Stare into its eyes. Stare into its eyes and hope to God it turned the fuck away.

Because if it didn't, he was screwed.

He was dead.

He thought back to the man they'd found in the woods. The way his body had been torn apart. The blue uniform he'd been wearing, and it all just clicked. The buggy. This was a safari park. Some kind of safari park.

And it was filled with a bucketload of starving animals.

The lion grunted as it stared at Hayden. Breathed heavily. Beautiful but terrifying, no doubt about that. And lying in the mud, staring at this lion, it felt like every other single sense evaded Hayden. A sense of where he was. Of who was around him. Of what he was going to do.

All he knew was that he had to get away.

He had to get away from this lion.

Somehow, he had to get away.

He heard a wince. Heard movement behind him to his right.

And a cough.

The lion turned. Looked in the direction of the cough, too.

Sarah.

Shit. Sarah. Regaining consciousness. She couldn't make a sound. Not now. Not—

The lion put one foot in front of the other, started to move.

Hayden's insides turned to mush. He knew right then that he had to move. That there was nothing else he could do. No way he could just stay put, no way he could hope the lion would turn away, disappear into the woods.

He had to run.

He had to get to Sarah, to Holly—wherever the hell she'd gone.

He had to get away.

He took a deep breath of the cool air, a smell of decomposition lingering.

He felt a trickle of sweat roll down his forehead.

You can do this, Hayden.

You can fucking do this.

He waited until the lion made another step. Another step towards Sarah, another step up the hill.

Then he turned around and he ran.

He didn't look back as he clambered up the hill, splashing around in the mud, trying to keep his balance. He just powered on. Saw Sarah. Saw her lying on the dirt beside the broken remains of the buggy. Holly was nowhere to be seen. She'd done a runner. Fuck. She could've helped but she'd done some kind of runner. He knew she wasn't to be trusted. Knew he had to keep an eye on her.

But shit.

He had other things to worry about right now.

He stuck his fingers in the mud and dragged himself up the side of the hill. His feet slipped with every step, and behind him he could hear the lion growling, hear its huge paws patting through the mud.

He imagined its teeth. Imagined it opening its cavernous mouth and closing in on Hayden. Ripping him to shreds, just like it had the man they found in the woods; just like it had all those other bodies they'd found in the woods.

He kept on running.

Still alive.

Still staring at Sarah, who looked out of it, grimacing in pain. Her arm looked dislocated, snapped out of its socket. Blood dripped from her nostrils.

But she was alive.

Just like Hayden, she was alive.

He heard the lion roar and he tasted sick at the back of his throat, felt his stomach rise into his chest, his heart pounding and pounding and pounding. But on he went. On he crawled through the mud. On he climbed towards Sarah. Because that's what he had to do—climb. Climb through the mud, one step at a time.

Deep breaths.

Keep his cool.

Keep his—

"Hey!"

He heard the voice above. Over to his left.

A familiar voice.

Holly's voice.

Hayden chanced a look and saw that Holly was holding a gun. Pointing it shakily at the lion. Fear all over her face.

But she was standing her ground.

Standing her ground as Hayden got closer to Sarah.

Got closer to helping her. Closer to saving her.

He didn't look over his shoulder. Couldn't let himself. Because he could tell from the fear on Holly's face that the lion was close. That it was still chasing him. That—

He felt his boot slip.

Felt the soft muddy ground give way underneath him.

And he fell face flat into the soil.

He scrambled to pull himself up as mud filled his eyes, as the bitter earthy taste engulfed his mouth. This was it. This was the moment the lion caught up with him. The moment this surreal fucking turn of events came to a conclusion. The moment it tore him apart—tore Sarah apart and put an end to both of them, piece by piece.

Holly had to fire the gun.

He didn't want to see a lion harmed, always stood against animal cruelty, but she just had to fire the gun.

He dragged himself up. Saw Holly still standing there, frozen. Still pointing the weapon. Sarah just a couple of metres away.

"Fire it!" Hayden shouted.

But she didn't.

Holly just kept standing there. Frozen. Rigid. Hands shaking.

The rest of the weapons lying in the rucksack beside the overturned buddy.

Hayden rushed over to Sarah. Wrapped his arms around her

and tried to lift her. She squealed when he pushed against her right side—when he hurt her dislocated shoulder.

"You—you have to get up," Hayden said. "I'm sorry but you have to get up—"

A force.

A force slamming into Hayden's back.

Smacking him deep into the mud, covering him with darkness.

Pressing down.

Pressing down hard.

He knew what it was. He knew what it was and he couldn't feel hard done by. Because he'd left Gary behind. He'd knocked Gary out and left him to die in the woods. Didn't matter if he'd made him unconscious. Didn't matter at all. All that mattered was he'd played God with someone else's life. He'd betrayed a companion.

And now he was going to pay for it.

Piece by agonising piece.

He searched the damp grass for something, anything.

Searched it for a rock. For something to hit the lion with. Something to bat it off.

Felt its sharp, uncut claws dig into his shoulder.

Its hot breath and slimy drool dripping all over his neck.

Its growl loud in his ears.

He searched.

Searched some more.

Then he felt something.

Felt something—the bag. The zip of the rucksack. The weapons rucksack.

He stuffed his fingers inside it, stuffed them in as far as he could stretch, as far as he could reach.

Desperate.

Determined.

And then he felt the tip of something sharp.

Felt the tip of something sharp nick his fingertips.

Grabbed it, as the lion pressed down harder, as its mane brushed against his neck.

Spun it around.

And swung it in the lion's direction as hard as he could.

He wasn't sure he'd had much success. Not at first. Because the lion was still pressing him down. Still holding him. Still breathing its rancid breath all over him.

And then he heard a whimper.

He heard a whimper and he felt hot blood and he pulled the blade away and stabbed it again.

Stabbed it and felt guilt, felt nothing but immeasurable guilt for what he was doing, as the lion cried, struggled.

Stabbed it and felt tears rolling down his cheeks as he fought off the hungry beast. The beast that was just trying to do the same as everyone else in this world—survive.

He stabbed it a third time and this time, the lion pulled away.

The weight shifted from Hayden's body.

He turned over. Rolled over, every inch of his body feeling infinitely lighter.

He scurried back. Sat beside Sarah. Looked back at the lion.

He expected it to be dying. To be toppled over onto its side. To be looking up at Hayden with fear. With confusion.

But it wasn't.

It was bleeding. Bleeding just between its ribs.

But it was standing.

It was alive.

It looked Hayden in his eyes, looked at him just as it had before, and then it turned away.

Turned away and limped off into the woods.

Into whatever fate awaited it.

Hayden put a hand around Sarah's back. Heart still racing. Adrenaline so rich it made him want to puke. The smell of sweat strong.

"Come on," he said. "Let's … let's get you up."

"Guys," Holly said. "I ... I'd hurry. If I were you. I'd hurry."

It was then that Hayden heard the growl.

Heard the muffled cries.

He turned and looked into the woods, looked between the branches where the lion had disappeared.

Saw it on its side.

Saw a mass of zombies surrounding it.

Sticking their teeth inside it.

Ripping its beautiful golden fur away.

He felt his eyes sting with tears. Felt guilt. Felt shame for what he'd had to do. For the only thing he'd been able to do to survive.

But that guilt was short-lived.

That sadness was short-lived.

Because he heard another growl behind him, behind Holly.

Turned and saw a lioness standing in the middle of the dirt track.

Staring down at her king being torn to shreds.

Staring at Holly, at Sarah, at Hayden.

Growling.

TWENTY

"Shoot, Holly. Just—just shoot."

Hayden didn't know what else to say. What else to suggest to Holly as the lioness approached her, crept up to her.

Behind him, at the bottom of the hill, the lion whimpered as the infected tore it apart.

And the lioness watched every bit of it.

But Holly's eyes were filling up. Hayden could see it from this far away, the partly conscious Sarah by his side. He could see the guilt in her eyes as she held onto the gun. As her hands shook.

He could see her love for this lioness.

That killing it was the last thing she wanted to do.

"I know it's hard," Hayden called, the sound of zombies ripping open the lion's belly splitting through the air. The stench of death strong, pertinent. "I know it's hard but you've just gotta—"

"I can't. I—"

"You have to," Hayden shouted. "You just ... you just have to."

He watched the lioness step closer to Holly.

Watched it move closer, closer, all the while the zombies

behind chewed up the poor lion, their attention destined to shift to Hayden, to Sarah in no time ...

"You have to—"

"I'm sorry," Holly said.

She lifted the gun.

Pointed it at the lioness.

And she pulled the trigger.

There was no explosion of blood from the lioness. No pained scream. No sudden anguished thud as its beautiful body fell to the ground.

Instead, the lion jumped aside.

Jumped away from Holly, fear in its eyes. Backing off. Stepping away.

"That's it," Hayden said, attempting to lift Sarah up, move towards Holly. "That's—that's it. Keep on—"

Holly fired again.

A bullet rattled into the grass, just in front of the dirt track.

The lioness moaned. Curled up its face and growled.

But still, as Holly pointed her gun at it, it backed away.

Backed away from Holly.

Backed away from the group.

Backed away from ...

It was then that Hayden heard the gasps behind him. That he heard the footsteps sloshing up the mud.

That he smelled the eye-watering stench of decay edging closer.

He turned. Didn't have to, but did anyway, just to see, just to know for certain.

"Shit," he said.

The crowd of zombies were rushing away from the emaciated corpse of the lion.

Staggering up the muddy hill.

Surging towards Hayden, Sarah, Holly.

"Better get the hell back on the dirt track," Holly said. "Grab—grab a gun. Grab whatever you can then ..."

She turned back to the lioness. Lifted her gun. Tilted her head forward in a sudden movement; a movement that made the lioness cower back, frightful of another blast. Under control.

For now.

Hayden rushed over to the weapons bag beside him. Grabbed two pistols, handed one to Sarah.

"You okay?"

She clung to her dislocated shoulder. Bit down on her lip. Nodded sharply—a nod that told Hayden in no uncertain terms that no, she wasn't okay. She was far from okay.

But she grabbed hold of the gun.

Stepped to her feet, slowly.

Bloodstains above her top lip. Clotting around her nostrils.

Sarah wasn't okay.

But for now, she was alive.

She was alive, and that was all that counted.

The pair of them moved up to the side of the dirt track, up the slippery mud and to Holly. Holly was still walking towards the lioness, gun raised. Still standing tall. Finger on the trigger. Ready to shoot at any given moment.

The lioness was backing away.

Looking at all of them—at Hayden, Sarah, Holly—and backing away.

Behind, the gasps of the zombies grew louder.

"Need to find a way out of here somehow," Hayden said.

"Up the dirt track," Holly said. "On the left."

She didn't turn. Didn't point.

Just kept her aim on the lioness.

Kept on stepping towards it.

Staring into its eyes.

Hayden frowned. Looked down the road. "What's—"

"There's a building down there. Through the trees. You see it?"

Hayden didn't want to look away from the lioness. Managed to chance a glance—just the briefest of glances.

Then he saw it.

Saw the building.

The grey brick designed to look like some unearthed rock.

Reptile's Domain.

His stomach turned. "Not sure I like the sound of that."

"Not sure I like the sound of those infected coming our way," Holly said. "Or this lioness' growling."

"How're—how're we supposed to make it there?" Sarah said.

Holly kept her gun pointed at the lioness.

Kept on looking it, staring it in the eye.

Then, "You run," she said. "I'll ... I'll hold off what I can."

Hayden's muscles tightened. "You—you can't just—"

"One of us has to."

"But you've been bitten. You've ... you've been bitten and you're alive. Which means we need you. Which means we—"

Hayden didn't get to finish.

He didn't get to finish because the lioness suddenly stopped.

Lifted its head.

Leaped at Holly.

Hayden watched it move through the air in slow motion. Watched its gorgeous fur contrast with the greying sky. Watched it move by in front of him, the sounds of the zombies drifting away, the smells of decay disappearing, nothing else mattering but the lioness, nothing else mattering but its beautiful form flying through the air at Holly.

Hayden started to lift his gun.

Started to aim.

Started to squeeze his trigger.

But he didn't have to.

Blood spurted out of the head of the lioness.

Its paws flailed in the air, its jump losing shape, its progression losing momentum.

Holly rolled out the way as the lioness landed in the mud, splattered down on the soft ground.

As its still, silent, peaceful body slid down the muddy hill towards the oncoming zombies.

The eternally hungry zombies.

Holly wiped her eyes. The pistol in her hand shook. She looked back at the lioness. Looked back at it as the zombies surrounded it. As they kneeled beside it. As they stuck their sharp fingers into its fur and ripped it open, just like they had the lion, just like they would with everything living—once living—on this earth.

Hayden and Sarah walked up to Holly.

Walked up to her as she stood there, tears rolling down her cheeks, staring back at the poor lioness as the rain started to fall.

"You did what you had to do," Hayden said.

He put a hand on her back.

Patted her.

"You saved us."

Then he walked past Holly. Walked up onto the dirt track. Walked with Sarah, back onto the road. The road they had to get off. The place they had to get out of.

For they had to push on to Holyhead.

They had to keep on moving.

"Come on," Hayden said. "We'd better move."

Holly stood there a few more seconds.

Stood there and stared at the feast. Stared at the mangled, bony hands stuffed inside the lioness' innards. At the lion in the distance, its mane covered in rich, red blood.

She stared at it and she didn't say a word, transfixed, grief-stricken.

Then, she turned.

Turned around and followed Hayden, followed Sarah.

And when she glanced into Hayden's eyes, Hayden wanted her to see the way he looked at her.

With belief.

With trust.

Because she'd put her life on the line.

She'd put her life on the line and done the only thing she could do to keep the group alive.

She stepped onto the dirt track.

Stood beside Sarah.

Looked back at Hayden.

She'd earned her place.

Earned a right to walk with them.

Earned their trust.

"You ready?" Hayden asked.

Sarah nodded.

Holly didn't do a thing. Not at first. Not right away.

Then she glanced at Hayden again.

Glanced, and nodded.

Together, the three of them walked.

Together, the three of them pushed on to Holyhead. Pushed on to whatever awaited.

Together, the three of them trusted.

BUT TRUST COULD BE the greatest deception.

TWENTY-ONE

You saved us.

Those three words echoed around Holly's mind as she walked with Hayden and Sarah. As they walked down the dirt track. As they snapped the necks of stray zombies that rushed at them, that launched themselves up the muddy hill at the side of the track desperate for a bite, eager to sink their teeth right in.

You saved us.

And maybe Hayden was right. Maybe Holly had saved him. Saved Sarah. Maybe she'd done a good deed. Gone against her morals killing the lioness. Stood against it, stood for the good of the group—for the survival of the group—and pulled the trigger to make sure the three of them survived.

You saved us.

Maybe she had.

But she had her reasons.

She had her motives.

She gripped the gun tightly in her hand as they made their way to the front gates of the safari park. On her left, Holly saw a rhino. Standing there, cutting a solitary figure, all alone with nobody to help it, nobody to feed it.

It stared back at her like it knew. Like it knew it was just like her.

Like it understood her secret.

Understood the truth.

She felt the wound on her left forearm twinge. The site of the bandage. The site of the bite.

She thought back to the dark cabin. How she'd sat inside there all alone, terrified to leave.

How she'd curled up in a ball as the world went to shit all around her.

As zombies marched through the streets.

As bombs fell from the sky.

She'd curled up in a ball and wished she was with Andy. Wished he was here with her to hold her hand. To tell her everything was going to be okay. To tell her they'd pull through this hell; both of them were strong and they'd pull through this hell.

She wished he was there with her, right then, and she wished he was here with her, right now.

But he wasn't.

He was in Holyhead.

And that's why Holly had to get to Holyhead.

That's why someone had to take her there.

Someone stronger than her.

Someone to protect her.

She looked at the bandage on her arm and remembered what she'd done. The gamble she'd took.

Sinking her teeth into her own skin.

Pressing down and fighting against the first barrier of pain. Fighting as the skin split, as the metallic taste of blood filled her mouth.

Fighting against the second barrier of pain as she reached the muscle. The raw muscle, rubbery like uncooked meat.

Fighting against the third barrier of pain as she kept a vice grip on her flesh. As she kept on pressing down, harder, firmer.

A risk.

A fake bite wound.

No. Not fake. Totally real. For it was a bite wound. She told everyone the truth about that. She had been bitten. She had survived. Made it this far.

She just didn't tell anyone who'd bitten her.

The source of the bite wound.

She just didn't tell anyone she'd done it to herself.

"You okay?"

Holly turned. Saw Hayden looking at her. Observing her closely as she walked with the group. Gun in her hand. Tight in her sweaty palms.

"Just ... just feel bad. For what I had to do."

She played the animal rights activist card.

Masked the truth.

The truth that she'd weighed up leaving Hayden and Sarah to be butchered by the lion.

That she'd turned. Tried to run. And if it weren't for the lioness, she'd be out of here.

But then the other sides of the scales weighed back down on her. Reminded her she was alone. She was without a vehicle. Her odds of making it all the way to Holyhead alone were slim at best, suicide at worst.

"We'll push on," Hayden said, specks of rain falling from the dark grey clouds. "Then we'll find somewhere. Somewhere to stay for a while. To take a break."

Holly feigned an exhausted smile.

Nodded.

It wasn't that she didn't like Hayden or Sarah. Wasn't that she had anything against them—anything against anyone she'd travelled this far with.

She just couldn't tell them the truth.

Because if she told them the truth, no one would walk with her. No one would travel to Holyhead with her. No one would protect her.

She'd made it this far.

So many people had died because of her, but she'd made it this far.

She turned and saw Sarah looking at her. Looking at her with that furrowed brow. That obvious suspicion all over her face.

If only she knew what she'd do to her.

She'd do anything.

If it meant getting to Andy.

Her Andy.

No one else's Andy.

They reached the gates of the safari park. Stood underneath the opening. Looked back at the vast expanse of grass, trees, land.

"Hopefully someone'll keep an eye on them," Hayden said, nodding at the gazelles. Gazelles chewing the grass—what little grass they hadn't already chewed. Oblivious to the truth. The truth that this was the end. That this was over. For them, for everyone, this was it.

But not for Holly.

Not for Andy.

She turned.

Walked out of the gates.

Walked onto the road, Sarah by her side, Hayden by her side.

You saved us.

Yes, she had saved them. They'd seen her save them. Seen her fight for them.

And that was perfect.

That was ideal.

That was what she needed.

But she knew what she had to do when she reached Holyhead.

Knew what she had to do if they made it that far—if somehow she didn't lose them just before she got there.

She tightened her grip on the gun.

Walked along the road.

She'd do what she had to do.

Do what she had to do to stop them punishing her.

Do what she had to do to stop them chastising her for her lie.

For the truth.

She looked at Hayden, looked at Sarah, and she thought about doing it. Thought about lifting her gun and killing them right here.

But then she saw the movement up ahead.

The movement of zombies.

More infected spilling out of the woods. Stepping onto the road.

So she lifted her gun.

Turned it at the infected.

Fired.

She'd kill Hayden and Sarah if she had to.

She didn't want to, but if she had to, she would.

Just not yet.

Not while there was still a journey ahead.

Not while Andy was still so, so far away.

She'd kill them.

She'd kill them when she had to.

Without hesitation.

She'd kill them.

Just not yet.

TWENTY-TWO

Hayden walked down the long empty road and wondered how long it'd be before he finally toppled over.

The sun beamed down from above but Hayden couldn't shake the feverish grip of cold that split through his bones. His throat was dry. Not a single sip of water since they'd lost the rucksack back at the safari park. His stomach churned with hunger. He imagined the spices of curry, the succulence of fresh chicken and fluffy rice ... things he used to enjoy in the old world. Things he'd eat as comfort food from the local Indian whenever he couldn't be arsed cooking.

Which, of course, turned out to be pretty frequent.

"Not sure I can walk much further," Sarah said.

Hayden looked at her. Looked at her as she staggered down the cracked concrete. Over the potholes in the road, crunching through the smashed shards of glass. She looked tired. Exhausted. Of course, all of them looked tired and exhausted, but Sarah. Her face, deathly pale. The patch of blood just above her top lip—the reminder of what had happened to her earlier, of her collapse.

The collapse she seemed eager not to talk about.

But the collapse they all had to address at some stage.

The words smeared in front of young Tim's body.

KAREN NOT BIT HES AIRBOURNE TIM AIR—

They made Hayden shudder.

Hayden walked over to Sarah. Held a hand out for her.

She raised her eyes. Narrowed them at him. A look that told him to piss off. That she was tough enough. That she could make it alone.

Hayden lowered his hand.

In truth, he was relieved.

Relieved 'cause he wasn't sure he'd be able to support the extra pressure.

Prop up the added weight.

"We'll get through this," Hayden said.

Sarah didn't look back at him. Not this time.

And he was glad about that too.

Because he wasn't totally sure he believed himself.

He turned. Looked ahead. Looked at Holly as she walked in front of Hayden, in front of Sarah. Led the way down the middle of the abandoned street. Boarded-up windows in red-bricked buildings either side of them. The sounds of cans scraping against the concrete in the wind.

Silence.

Deathly silence.

Silence Hayden had learned not to trust.

"Better go see to her," Hayden whispered.

Sarah gave him that sideward glance. The one she always gave when it came to Holly. He knew Sarah didn't like her. Knew there was a distance between the pair of them. A mistrust.

And while Hayden had his guard up—while he had his guard up about everyone—he saw no reason to doubt Holly. She'd come so far with them. Put her neck on the line to keep them alive. That had to count for something.

Right?

He stepped forward. Tried to jog but fuck, his knees weren't in the mood right now.

"You okay?" Hayden asked.

Holly kept on looking straight ahead. Kept on focusing on the road in the distance. The sun lighting up her pale face.

"Holly, are you—"

"We need to talk. About … about Sarah."

She whispered Sarah's name. Glanced back over her shoulder. Sarah just looked on. Stared on.

"What about her?" Hayden asked.

"You know what. You told me what happened. To—to the kid back at Riversford. To your friends."

"And what's that got to do with—"

"You know exactly what it's got to do with the kid," Holly said, raising her voice a little. She looked at Hayden now. Looked right into his eyes. "Sarah. If—if she's … if the virus is airborne then she's a danger."

"Then what're you suggesting?"

"I'm suggesting we do the right thing. The kindest thing. For everybody."

It was those final words that lifted Hayden's defences. That made him uncertain. That gave him an overriding bad feeling. A crippling dread.

"So that's what you do, is it? Leave people behind when they're no good?"

"Oh don't start—"

"We didn't leave you behind. We took you in. Could've left you out there. Could've left you to die outside those walls. But we didn't."

"No. No you just left Gary to die instead."

Hayden stumbled, and he knew he'd made a bad move in doing so right away.

His throat welled up.

Dread and guilt scratched inside his head.

"I know what happened back there," Holly said, staring at Hayden. "I've seen the guilt in your eyes. I've seen that guilt so many times in so many people. I know what it looks like."

Hayden's lips felt like elastic. "You—you don't know—"

"You keep on telling yourself you didn't do anything wrong. That you're innocent here. You keep on telling yourself you've never sacrificed somebody to preserve your own survival."

She looked away. Looked right at the ground. Scratched at the bandage on her arm, the bandage on her bite wound.

"You keep telling yourself that," she said.

Hayden wanted to respond. He wanted to come back with something confident. Something assertive. Something to put Holly in her place.

But he couldn't.

He was too tired to come back.

Too weak.

Too guilty.

He wanted to say something to Holly, to make sure she knew she wasn't the one who called the shots around here. That she was here because Hayden kept her alive. Because Sarah kept her alive. Because Hayden's people, they'd trusted her. They all trusted her.

He wanted to argue with her assertion that everyone had sacrificed somebody.

That everyone was guilty of something.

He wanted to, but then he heard the thud.

Heard the crack against the road behind them.

He looked over his shoulder and he saw Sarah lying face flat on the concrete.

Blood pooling out of her nostrils.

Seeping through the cracks in the road.

And behind her, creeping around the side roads and out into the street, out towards them, infected.

TWENTY-THREE

"Quick!"

Hayden rushed as fast as he could towards Sarah's fallen body. He didn't know whether she was alive. Whether she was dead. Just that she'd collapsed. She'd fallen on the road. Passed out again.

He didn't know what her fate was. Didn't know whether she'd tripped from this plane of existence already. Whether his efforts were in vain.

All he cared about was getting to her.

Saving her.

Making sure he got to her before the infected.

He tried to run but his legs were weak and stiff. But he pushed on through the pain. Pushed through the stiffness. And even though Sarah was only a few metres away, it felt like she was a mile or more.

Even though the zombies were still just in the distance, even though they were scattered into smaller groups, it felt like they were much, much closer.

So close that Hayden felt surrounded.

"Holly!" Hayden shouted. Didn't look back. Just knew he

needed her help. Needed her help to lift Sarah. To get her on her feet. "Need a fucking hand here!"

But then, as he reached Sarah's side, the conversation he'd just had with Holly flashed into his mind.

The talk about sacrifice.

About leaving people behind if it meant self-preservation.

How that's all Hayden had done with Gary. How that was the real reason he hit him across the head, left him for dead.

Because he knew downing Gary could keep him alive.

He'd knocked him out because he didn't want Gary to suffer, didn't want him to experience any pain.

But he'd knocked him out because saving Gary meant sacrificing himself.

And in this new world, nobody sacrificed themselves.

Not when they knew what awaited.

He crouched down beside Sarah. Felt rain peppering down from the greying clouds above. "Sarah."

He put a hand on her shoulder and went to turn her over but she just flopped to her side. Rolled, limp and unconscious and still.

Blood still pooling out of her nostrils.

And her ears.

And her eyes.

He heard the gasps up ahead. Heard the growls and the cries getting closer, the rain powering down against the concrete. He looked up. Saw two zombies at the front of the group. One was dressed in a white shirt and black trousers, its white shirt torn at the side, a chunk missing from its torso. The second one was shorter, skinnier. A teenager perhaps. Teenage girl. Barbie-doll hair. Long, fake blue nails.

Dragging her intestines along with her, trying not to trip on them.

"Come on," Hayden said, reaching down for Sarah, trying to

lift her. But he couldn't. His muscles just couldn't support her weight, not completely. He needed help. "Holly! Please!"

He looked over his shoulder and he saw the look on Holly's face.

It was a look Hayden imagined he'd had when he was debating what to do with Gary. When he was deciding whether to leave him in the woods to die or whether to fight. Fight to save him. Go down fighting if he had to.

It was a look that terrified him.

But a look he knew many would've had since the world went to shit.

"Please, Holly. I—We need you here. We need you."

"It's over," Holly said. "She's—she's gone. Just... Come on, Hayden. Come—"

"She's not gone. She needs your help. I need your help."

"It's worthless." Rain poured down now. Drenched Holly. Made it look like tears were dripping down her face. "You—you know it is. You have to leave her."

"I won't fucking leave her," Hayden said.

He turned back to Sarah. Put his arms under her body and tried, tried with all he had to drag her up, to lift her, to pull her away.

All the while, the zombies got closer.

The infected approached.

Hungry.

Ready for another sacrifice.

And it was at that moment, as Hayden looked up at the zombies, trying his damnedest to lift Sarah, that Holly's words resonated with him. That he understood the true test was ahead.

As the infected inched closer, just a few metres away now, Hayden asked the question.

Can I stay with her?

Can I sacrifice myself trying to save her?

Am I capable of doing that?

"Hayden, please," Holly shouted.

Hayden didn't respond. He didn't say a word back to Holly.

Instead, he reached into his pocket with his shaking hand.

Lifted out the gun. The gun they'd promised to preserve the ammo of in case of emergency. Well this was an emergency. It was an absolute fucking emergency.

Sarah's life was worthy of an emergency.

He let the white-shirted infected step within an inch of him and then he fired.

Fired right at its throat. Hoped for a clean shot—a shot at its neck, a bullet to sever its spinal cord.

But the zombie just staggered back.

Staggered back, bleeding, into its companion.

But still standing.

Still looking at him.

And then walking towards him again.

"Hayden you've got to—"

"No!" Hayden said.

He stood his ground.

Stood above Sarah.

Pulled the trigger again, the sound of the gunshot echoing against the walls of the buildings.

Because he wasn't leaving Sarah.

He wasn't leaving anyone else behind.

He couldn't allow himself to leave anyone else behind.

And yet that voice whispering in the back of his mind got louder and more prominent when the second bullet did nothing to put the zombie down.

When the second zombie stepped in front of the first, more zombies closing in from behind, their decomposing stench hanging in the air, the sound of buzzing flies deafening.

I won't let go.

He fired the trigger again.

I won't leave your side.

And again.

I won't …

He fired the trigger again but this time, nothing happened.

Nothing fired.

He was out.

All fucking out.

And all the infected were still standing.

Hayden looked into the eyes of the infected, looked at their eyes glistening in the rain and he knew what was going to happen. He knew what *had* to happen.

He was supposed to stand here with Sarah.

Fight with his fists if he had to for his friend. For someone who'd stood by his side. For someone he cared about.

But Holly's words echoed through his mind.

"You keep on telling yourself you've never sacrificed somebody to preserve your own survival."

He watched the infected walk closer.

Listened to the throaty snarls, the guttural cries.

He looked into their bloodshot eyes and he wanted to stay put.

To stand his ground.

But Sarah was still.

She was still. She'd bled out. Internal bleeding in her skull. Infected, even.

She was badly sick. As good as gone.

So Hayden had to do the only thing he could do.

The thing he didn't want to do, but the only thing possible.

"I'm so sorry," he said.

He looked down at Sarah. Looked at her, eyes closed and oblivious as rain dripped down her hair.

And then he took a step back.

But when he stepped back, he walked into something.

"Not just yet," Holly said.

She stepped around Hayden and smacked the first zombie

across the neck with a large piece of concrete from the cracked road.

Snapped its neck in one hit.

And then she swung at the next one. The skinny girl. Split her rotting skin, sent her flying to the ground.

And when she fell to the ground, Holly stepped over the girl and crushed her spinal cord.

Silenced her, once and for all.

She turned around, dripping rain and blood. "Better get a fucking move on then hadn't we?"

Hayden still couldn't believe it, still couldn't understand how close he'd come to walking away from Sarah.

But he didn't have time to dwell because more zombies were flooding towards them.

He rushed over to Sarah's body.

Crouched down by her side, fighting the fatigue, the hunger, the agony.

Holly got to Sarah's other side. Rain lashing down now. Making visibility difficult. "On three," she said. "One ..."

Memories of Gary flashed through Hayden's mind.

"Two ..."

Leaving him behind to die. To save himself.

"Three!"

Hayden lifted.

He lifted and Holly lifted.

He thought he felt something split in his lower back. Something crack. Expected his body to tumble down like a Jenga tower.

But it didn't.

He was on his feet.

Holly was on her feet.

Sarah was in their arms.

"Where now?" Hayden asked.

Holly looked over her shoulder. The dozen or so infected still staggering their way. Still growling at them. Still getting ready to feed.

"Anywhere but here," she said.

And then, Sarah in their arms, the pair of them walked.

They walked, but Hayden couldn't shake the image.

Couldn't shake the emotion he'd felt when he stood over Sarah's body.

The temptation to just walk away. To just leave.

He wanted Sarah to move. Wanted her to make a sound. Just something to give him a sign that she was okay. That she was hanging on in there.

But she didn't.

She didn't move a muscle.

Blood dripped from her orifices and down Hayden's coat, down onto the road.

A reminder of the bloodshed he'd nearly caused.

Of a friend he'd almost given up on.

Again.

TWENTY-FOUR

When Hayden and Holly rushed inside the partly-open garage door, Sarah still hadn't moved a muscle. They climbed underneath the doorway. Into the darkness, into the dust. Knew it was risky. Knew there was every chance a group of zombies would be waiting inside, just waiting to tear them apart.

But anywhere was better than outside.

Outside with the approaching infected.

Outside, with certain death following their every step.

"You got it?" Hayden asked.

Holly pulled the handle of the garage door. Tensed. Pressed all her weight against it.

"I'll give you a—"

Hayden didn't need to help Holly out.

The garage door slammed shut.

Darkness filled the garage.

There was complete silence for a few moments. Nothing but the rattling echo of the garage door. Of the heavy breathing of Holly. Listening for a groan. A gasp. A sign of life—or death—inside this garage.

Something they could do without right now.

Something they could do without forever.

"How is she?" Holly asked.

Hayden leaned over Sarah, squinting and trying to get a better view in the darkness. The tiniest of openings in the metal garage door gave him the slightest bit of visibility, but it wasn't great. "Could do with some night-vision goggles."

"I'll let you know if I find any lying about."

"Good luck with that."

He pressed his hand against Sarah's chest and prepared for the worst. She was still. She was silent. She had been silent for so, so long.

But he had to hope. He had to hope she'd pull through.

He wasn't going to give up on her.

He'd almost given up on her and he hadn't liked the feeling it gave him then. The intense guilt. The self-loathing.

No. He was going to fight. He was going to fight for her with everything he had.

Because that's what he was now: a fighter.

Not a self-defender, but a fighter.

And he'd do everything he could to make sure those around him didn't fall.

"Feel a pulse?" Holly asked, her voice making Hayden jump.

Hayden waited. Held his shaky hands against her chest. Then moved his fingers to her wrist. Looked for a sign. Always had been shitty at first aid, that kinda thing. Hadn't really needed it in his life at all in truth. Not something that had ever come in handy.

Could've done with some advanced knowledge right now.

Or even some basic knowledge would've been nice.

He moved his fingers around Sarah's soft wrist. Her skin felt ... different. Like the difference between a stuffed animal and a real animal. Nothing radically different in appearance, sure. But just a *feeling*. A feeling that something was wrong. A sense that something was amiss; something was off.

Sarah felt like the stuffed animal right now.

"I ... I can't—"

"Did you hear that?"

Hayden hadn't. He hadn't heard a thing. "What?"

Holly was quiet.

"Holly? What—"

"Ssh."

"What did—"

And then Hayden heard it.

The clattering.

The footsteps.

"I think there's someone in here with us," Holly said.

Hayden listened. Listened some more. Nothing but silence now. No clattering. No footsteps.

"You want to check it out?" Holly asked.

Hayden thought about saying yes. Thought about responding. Telling Holly to stay here with Sarah.

But he'd made a vow.

Made a vow to himself never to let anyone go.

Never to turn his back on anyone again.

But also, never to let anyone put themselves at risk for his own survival.

"No."

"I'll go—"

"No," Hayden said. "We stay here. Until we—"

"Until we what?"

Hayden looked down at Sarah. Looked down at her body. Her paling skin almost luminous in the slightest of light.

"I'll go, Hayden. I can look after myself. Certainly did a decent job looking after you back there on the road."

Hayden thought back to the way he'd stepped back from Sarah. The way he'd given up. The way he'd *listened* to Holly and walked away.

"Thanks," he said.

"Don't have to thank me," Holly said, standing, kicking up dust.

"No. I do. For ... for Sarah. You didn't have to ... to come back. You didn't have to help. But you did. Thank you."

Holly didn't respond.

And Hayden couldn't see how her face changed in this darkness. Couldn't gauge her reaction.

She just crept away into the back of the room.

Into the unknown.

Hayden turned back to Sarah. Put a hand on her forehead. Cold. So icy cold he had to pull it away in an instant. He moved his hand down to her neck. Tried to feel a heartbeat. But it was difficult. Difficult with the numbness of his hands. With the fever running through his body.

He put his hand on Sarah's neck and he felt it.

Not the movement of a heartbeat.

But a sudden twitch.

A twitch of the muscle in her neck.

Hayden moved his hand away. His stomach turned to mush. His heart picked up. If this was it—if this was the moment Sarah came back—then he had to do what he had to do. He had to put her out of her misery.

And then he knew he'd probably end up joining her. Because if Sarah turned then the virus was airborne. It'd pass on to him. On to Holly. On to ...

"Hayden?"

He heard the voice and at first he thought it was Holly. But it came from underneath him. Yet it couldn't be Sarah. Because Sarah was unconscious. She was unconscious and—

"Hayden? Is ... is that you?"

But it was Sarah's voice.

Sarah was talking to him.

Sarah was alive.

He reached down. Wrapped his arms around her. Squeezed

her tight, not caring about whether the virus was airborne or not, not caring about anything other than Sarah being alive.

She'd pulled through.

She'd made it.

"Ow," she said. "Shoulder still …"

"Sorry," Hayden said, backing away. He wiped a tear from his face. "Sorry. I just—"

"What happened? Where—where are we?"

"It's—it's okay," Hayden said, adrenaline rushing through his system, still unable to believe Sarah was alive. That she'd made it. Pulled through. "It's okay. That's all that matters. It's—"

"Hayden," Holly said.

Her voice came from behind.

Echoed through the darkness.

He turned. Looked over to where she was. At least, where he thought she was.

Saw her faint silhouette in the darkness.

"She's made it," Hayden said. "Sarah, she's made it."

Holly didn't say anything.

Not for a moment.

Then, "There's something … something over here. Something you need to see. Right now."

TWENTY-FIVE

Hayden wasn't sure what to expect when Holly told him he needed to see something.

But when he saw it—when he understood exactly what it was she wanted him to see—the sense of dread and fear lifted.

In its place, hope emerged.

"Bit dusty, but looks in decent shape," Holly said. "I reckon it'll do the trick."

Hayden looked ahead. Squinted in the darkness.

The metal.

The glass.

The tyres.

A car.

"What about petrol? Stuff like that?"

Holly tutted. "It's a garage, Hayden. If a garage has one thing in abundance, it's petrol."

"And cold pasties," Hayden added.

Holly narrowed her eyes as she opened the car door, leaned inside. "Yeah. Those too."

Hayden and Sarah walked around the other side of the car.

Silver Honda Civic. Hard to tell the condition in the darkness, but it seemed in good nick.

It smelled fresh inside. Like fresh leather. A new car smell. Not a smell Hayden was too accustomed to having never learned to drive, but a smell he'd experienced in plenty of other cars over the years. His mum's cars. His dad's cars. His sister's cars. His old friends' cars.

Everyone's but his.

Holly sat in the driver's seat. Searched around for a key, for something to get the car started, to get it up and running. By Hayden's side, Sarah stood. She was weak. Shaky. But she was standing. She was standing and she was alive and that was something.

That was everything.

"Weird obsession with The Corrs," Holly said, leafing through the CDs in the glove compartment.

"What's up with The Corrs?" Hayden asked.

Holly side glanced at him. "I'll pretend you never asked that question."

"There's—there's some keys," Sarah said.

Her voice surprised Hayden. Startled Holly too by the looks of things.

Hayden looked at her. "What d'you mean there's—"

"Over by the door," Sarah said, raising a hand and pointing across the room. "There's ... there's a bundle. Over there. See."

Hayden looked over at where Sarah was pointing. Didn't see anything. Not at first.

And then he saw them.

Saw the keys dangling from the cork board through the smashed frosted glass of an office door.

Waiting for someone to pick them up.

Waiting for the group to take them.

Luring them in their direction ...

"I'll go," Holly said, climbing towards the car door.

"No," Hayden said. "I've ... I've got this."

"But I thought you—"

"In and out. As quickly as that."

He started to walk towards the door, away from Holly and Sarah before either of them could protest some more.

"The noise," Holly said. "The ... the noise we heard before."

She didn't turn it into a question. Didn't have to. Hayden got the suggestion.

But still he kept on walking.

"I'll be back in no time. You just ... just make sure that the car doesn't go slipping through our fingers."

He tensed his fists.

Walked closer and closer to the door.

When he reached it, he heard glass crunch under his feet. Something else, too. Something slippery. Something damp.

He didn't have to look at the floor to know that it was blood.

He just had to get through that door.

Get the keys.

Get out.

He held his breath and he reached up to the door. Pushed it open as gently as he possibly could, desperate not to make it creak, eager and determined to resist alerting anyone—anything —to his presence.

The door opened up.

Made the slightest squeak as it moved on its rusting hinges.

And then the keys were just metres away.

Just metres away, nothing stopping Hayden reaching them.

He wanted to just rush over to them, to snatch them from the wall and get the hell out of here. But he knew he had to be calm. He knew he had to keep his cool.

Because he had heard something earlier.

He'd heard something. And he knew what hearing something meant in this world. What it likely was.

He had to stay calm.

He had to stay focused.

He had to—

A sound.

A sound to his right.

Glass cracking.

He spun around. Looked into the darkness.

But no amount of squinting could help.

Too dark.

Too dark to see.

Too dark to know.

His heart racing, he turned back to the cork board. Walked. Just had to make it to the keys. Get to them. Get out of here. Didn't matter if there was something in the room with him. Didn't matter at all. He could leave it. He could get to the keys before it got to him.

He grabbed the bundle of keys dangling from the cork board.

Turned around.

He felt it before he saw it.

Felt the contact; the contact with *something*.

And then he knew exactly what it was when it pushed him back against the wall.

When it growled.

When he felt its dry skin, smelled its rotting flesh.

The zombie pressed him further into the wall. Hayden pushed back, pushed back with all the strength he had, but the zombie just kept on pressing.

Its face unrecognisable in the darkness.

Its skin cracking under Hayden's grip.

Its teeth getting closer, closer ...

Hayden lifted the heavy bundle of keys and pressed them against the zombie's neck. Pushed as far as he could into its throat.

And as he did, he could feel the zombie's skin giving way.

Feel it splitting apart like the skin of a grape left out in the sun.

He could feel dampness dribbling down his fingers.

Feel skin giving way to flesh.

Flesh giving way to bone.

And although the zombie kept on pushing, although it got closer, Hayden knew he wasn't far off.

Far off ripping the zombie's head from its shoulders.

Far off putting it down.

Far off—

He heard a splat from ahead, felt a whoosh of wind.

Then the zombie went limp.

Hayden pulled his blood-soaked hands away. The bundle of keys still in his grip.

The zombie dropped to the floor, head dangling on by a thread.

Behind it, Sarah stood. Shaky, no doubt weak, but holding a rusty wrench.

"A 'help me' wouldn't've gone amiss," she said, her voice quivery. But *alive*. Alive. "Now come on. Rather not stick around this place."

Hayden followed Sarah out to the car. Handed Holly the keys. Climbed inside the passenger door, letting Sarah take the back seat.

"Now's where we pray," Holly said, sticking the Honda key in the lock.

Turning the key.

The wait. The silent wait. For what felt like eternity.

And then ...

The engine coughed to life.

Holly whooped. Sarah clapped, patted Hayden's shoulder.

But Hayden didn't say a thing.

Didn't feel an ounce of celebration.

Because more zombies were staggering out of the back room.

More of them were crawling towards the car.

Too many of them.

"Better move quick," he said, and right on cue, Holly put her foot down, accelerated 'til they reached the garage door. "Half a fucking tank too! That'll do us just nicely—"

"The garage door," Sarah said. And then she looked behind. Looked at the zombies staggering towards the car just a matter of metres away. "D'we have time?"

Hayden waited at first.

Waited, tried to figure out the best option.

Could only arrive at one.

"More time now than we'll have in a second," he said.

He grabbed the wrench.

Then he climbed out of the passenger door.

Grabbed the bottom of the metal garage door.

And with all his strength, as the cries of the zombies echoed behind, he lifted.

It didn't budge at first. And for a moment Hayden started to wonder whether this was it. Whether this was where he died. Trying to save his group. Trying to help his friends.

Trying, and failing.

Then something clicked and the garage door raised.

At first Hayden felt nothing but relief as the bright light of outside filled the pitch-black garage.

He felt nothing but accomplishment.

Then he saw the crowd of zombies surrounding the garage entrance.

Dozens of them.

Watching.

Waiting.

Walking.

TWENTY-SIX

"Get the fuck back here! Quick!"

Hayden knew he had to move. He knew he had to get back to the car. He knew that if he didn't, he'd be surrounded. Torn to pieces. Devoured.

But all he could do was stare out the open garage door at the mass of zombies staggering his way.

Listen to the throaty snarls of the ones inside the garage.

The ones that'd stayed so silent earlier.

The ones that'd come out of nowhere.

"Hayden!" Sarah shouted.

Hayden tasted rot in the air. His heart pounded. Sweat dripped down his forehead. The zombies outside were still a good ten, nine metres away. But soon they'd be onto him. And then they'd be onto the car.

And together, inside the car, the three of them would be crushed.

Crushed under the weight of an unstoppable mass of solid flesh.

"Hayden—"

"Drive," he shouted.

Silence from Holly. Silence from Sarah.

Then, "What the fuck d'you mean?"

"I mean 'drive'," Hayden said, turning and looking at Sarah and Holly through the dusty car window. "No way any of us are gettin' out of a mass of zombies like this."

"But you can't—"

"I have—have to try something. Something to ... to clear our path."

"That's suicide," Sarah shouted.

"Maybe so," Hayden said.

He heard the words echo in his mind.

Drowning out the groans of the infected.

Maybe so.

It was suicide. Signing his own death warrant. Calling time on his own fucking existence all for the survival of others.

But that's what he had to do.

That's what he owed to Holly, to Sarah.

For what he'd done to Gary.

For leaving Gary behind.

"Hayden just get in the car and we'll ... Hayden!"

Hayden didn't get in the car.

He ran to his right.

The wall of zombies on his left.

Closing in.

Getting closer, closer ...

Death staring him in the eye. Literal death.

He ran down the pavement at the side of the infected-filled road. He didn't hear the engine rev up behind him. Didn't hear Holly or Sarah making their escape. Didn't hear anything. All he heard was the song of the dead. The hungry cries of their rotting forms.

Cries that grew louder.

Closer.

Cries that would soon engulf him.

And as he ran down the pavement, sun beaming down between the grey clouds, Hayden didn't feel fear anymore. Didn't feel afraid. He just felt sad. Sad that this was what his life had come to. After all the sacrifices he'd made and all the hell he'd gone through—losing his parents, losing Clarice—this was where his life ended.

He wouldn't even know if he'd left a mark on anybody. Wouldn't even know if the actions he'd done in the best interests of others would remain strong in the memory.

Destined to die.

Destined to be forgotten, just like everyone else.

He saw the zombie drift out of the doorway up to his right and he knew now was the time.

He turned. Saw the mass of zombies following him. Saw them staring at him with their dead eyes; eyes as lifeless as Action Men figurines.

But he saw they were scattered.

They weren't a mass. Not anymore. There was room. Room for the car to get through. Room for it to drive out of.

Room for Sarah and Holly to get away.

And really, that was all that mattered now.

Not himself. Not anything else.

Just doing what he had to do to save his friends.

But he wasn't going out without a fight.

He ran at the zombie stumbling out of the door and cracked the wrench against the back of its neck. It made a coughing sound, like it was choking on some foreign object, and then Hayden smacked the wrench into its neck again and it didn't make a sound anymore.

He turned. Saw the zombies closing in on him just a matter of feet away. Four of them, all bigger and bulkier than him, real close.

The first he'd have to fight.

The first he'd have to deal with.

He calmed his breathing, gripped the wrench and then he stepped forward.

Pummelled it into the skull of the first zombie.

Shattered it on impact.

The zombie tumbled down. Fell flat onto the road. Still wriggling. Still writhing. But down. That's all that mattered now—that it was down.

He'd finish it later.

When he'd finished the other three stepping his way.

The other six behind them.

He tried not to let the fear inside as he slammed the wrench into the neck of the next infected. As he cracked it across the temple of the next one, smashed the teeth of the next.

And the worst part was all those zombies were still living, in their undead sort of way. All of them hadn't been killed, not completely. Their spinal cords were still intact.

But Hayden didn't have time to finish them.

Just had to take down more of them.

Just had to dodge the ones on the ground.

Just had to hope for the best.

It was when he saw the chubby, curly-haired woman hurtling towards him that he knew his days were numbered.

He lifted his wrench.

Waited for her to arrive—for her to throw her immense weight into his chest.

Knock him on the road where the remains of the downed infected snatched away at his flesh.

No.

He had to stand his ground.

He had to ...

He saw it in an instant. In an instant that trickled to slow motion.

The car.

The silver Honda driving around the back of the zombies.

The infected all clawing at it, turning their attention to it, trying to reach it.

Sarah at the window.

"Quick!" she shouted.

Hayden saw it.

Saw the gap.

The chance to run.

The chance trickling away with every second.

The gap filling up with more zombies, more infected, his chances of survival drifting away.

He saw the fat woman lunging at him and he ducked.

He ducked, stepped to the right, and then he ran.

He kept his focus on the car as he sprinted at it with all his strength. His heart pounded. His legs were weak. Either side of him, zombies tried to grab him.

But he couldn't look at them.

Only at the car.

He felt their nails scratching at his body.

Felt the dust filling his nostrils, making him want to cough and heave and stop running.

But he couldn't.

He had to run.

All he could do.

Car just a metre away.

Car just—

And then he felt a hand grab his shirt.

The back door of the car opening.

Felt his shirt ripping away, the cotton tearing as a zombie clutched onto it.

"Come on!"

He ran against the force. Ran into the tear. Ran towards the open door, towards the car, towards the back seat.

And then something happened.

Something he wasn't expecting.

The car moved.

The back door slammed.

And as more zombies grabbed hold of him, as more of them filled the gaps in the road and ripped at his shirt, Hayden watched the car drive away.

Watched it disappear.

And through the back window, he saw Sarah looking back at him.

Shouting.

Slamming her hands against the glass.

And then the car was gone.

TWENTY-SEVEN

Even surrounded by a mass of zombies, Hayden wasn't sure he'd ever felt so alone.

He smacked the wrench into the foreheads of the infected gathered around him. His torn shirt dangled from his body, the cold and the rain seeping through onto his skin. He wanted to put the zombies down, but he didn't have time to.

He had to follow the car.

He had to push on to Holyhead.

He had to hope.

He kept his focus on the dip in the road. The dip Holly had driven the car over. And he thought about Sarah. Thought about the way she'd looked back at him. The way she slammed her palms on the glass.

He'd been close. So close to the car door. Inches from the car door.

And Holly had put her foot down.

Hayden couldn't explain why. Couldn't understand why. Maybe Holly had panicked. Maybe she'd seen the infected getting closer and she'd just panicked. Decided Hayden wasn't worth fighting for. Proven the very things she'd told Hayden—the things about leaving people behind, about being forced to leave people behind if she absolutely had to; if anyone absolutely had to.

But she didn't have to. That was the thing. There was no reason for her leaving Hayden behind.

She'd just put her foot down when she was so close to saving him and she'd gone.

Hayden heard the gasps behind him. Heard the splat of loose flesh as it dropped to the road. He didn't look over his shoulder. Didn't look back at the dead mass following. Only up the road. Ahead.

Because that's all he could do now. Focus on the road ahead.

Holly was gone.

Sarah was gone.

For whatever reason, both of them were gone, and Hayden was alone.

He tried to pick up his pace at first. Tried to run. But not only was he exhausted, he was worried, too. Worried about wasting energy. Worried about running out of fuel right when he needed it.

Worried about the inevitable, the unavoidable.

Death.

But there was nothing he could do about it. No good in moping.

Moping got nobody anywhere but killed.

So he just had to run.

He felt the dehydration kicking in when he'd walked for a good hour, maybe longer. Or maybe less than that. Hard to tell when you were alone. Hard to tell when the constant groans of zombies echoed against the walls of the buildings either side of you.

All he knew was he needed a rest.

He needed a break, somewhere.

He needed strength.

But he had to keep moving.

He walked past abandoned cars. Smashed windows in the front, blood painting the steering wheels. A selfish part of him wanted to find Holly's car. Wanted to find it stalled and broken down in the middle of this place. Didn't want either of them to be safe until he was safe too.

But he didn't find the silver Honda Civic.

Found lots and lots of abandoned cars, bodies inside some of them—men, women, children, animals—found lots and lots of blood.

But no Holly. No Sarah.

He staggered across the cracked concrete. His head starting to spin. Throat as dry as sandpaper. And he knew he was wrong for wishing Holly and Sarah hadn't got away without him. He didn't *mean* that, not really. Just he couldn't face it. Couldn't face this chastising. Couldn't bear to think that he was worthless all along. That he was still just the layabout letdown he'd always been. That he hadn't changed, not one bit, in spite of what happened with his home town, with his parents, with his sister.

He couldn't bear to look the old version of himself in the eye and accept that's who he still was.

Because no.

He wasn't.

He was a fighter now.

And he was going to fight to Holyhead.

He was going to fight with all he had.

The thought just entered his mind when he saw the movement up ahead.

The first zombie looked easy enough to handle. White shirt pasted in blood. Thin black hair filled with dirt. Constant snarl on its face.

But handcuffs were wrapped around its chapped, worn wrists.

Hayden took a step towards it, gripped his hammer and readied to put it down when he saw the other zombies emerge from behind it.

It was at that moment Hayden realised exactly what the scene of this wreck was. A police van. One of the big blue ones that the S.W.A.T teams use—well, not S.W.A.T, whatever the UK equivalent was, he'd never needed to check. Didn't matter.

What mattered were the pile of police officers stumbling out of it.

In varying stages of decomposition.

Kitted out in full body armour, helmets included.

"Fuck." Hayden looked to the left. Looked at the rickety old building. Tried to figure out if he could make it in there, then make it out the other side perhaps. But it looked dark in there. Dark and dusty. Not somewhere he wanted to lock himself inside. Not knowing the horrors that lurked in the darkest of places. Not knowing the reality of unlocked doors in the new world.

But there wasn't much he could do about it.

The armoured zombies were coming for him.

So he had to do something.

He ran over to this building on his left. Grabbed the handle of the front door, turned it.

It wasn't an unlocked door.

And neither was the one beside it.

Or the one beside that.

He heard the groans getting closer. Looked over his shoulder and saw the infected were in the middle of the lane now. Blocking his way out. Meaning his only choice was this building. His only choice was one of the doorways or one of the windows …

Yes. The windows. That's what he had to try.

He rushed over to the window, heart pounding, and he pulled his wrench back.

He stopped when he saw what was behind it.

Four zombies.

All crouched over a fly-covered carcass of a woman.

Ribs poking out of her body, through her skin, still yet to turn.

All of them feasting.

He heard the snarl behind him.

So close. Closer than he'd originally thought.

And he tried to move to the right. Tried to run.

But he couldn't.

Another six zombies coming his way.

More of them swarming the road.

Crowding the area.

Surrounding him.

As he held his breath and his wrench, Hayden looked at the oncoming zombies and wondered whether this was it. Whether this was finally the moment his time ran out. And whether that was even such a bad thing anymore now that he was stranded, alone.

No.

He didn't give up. Not anymore.

He fought.

He lifted his wrench and prepared to crack it across the neck of the first infected.

But there was no first infected.

There were ten of them.

So he picked one. Focused on one. Ignored the ones around it. Prepared himself.

He'd fight.

He'd fight to the end.

He'd—

A smash.

A cracking of bones.

The smell of engine fumes, of petrol.

And then an opening, right in the middle of the road.

A car.

A silver Honda Civic.

"Get the fuck inside, quick!"

Sarah.

Sarah shouting for Hayden.

He blinked. She couldn't be here. Holly, Sarah, they couldn't be back for him. They couldn't—

"We ain't coming back for you again," Holly shouted. "Get the fuck in the car right this second."

Hayden watched the infected drift between him and the car.

Watched them fill the gap.

He held the wrench as tightly as he could.

Lifted it.

Because he was a fighter.

He'd always fight, now.

Not just for himself, but for everyone.

Just like they fought for him.

And then, he ran.

TWENTY-EIGHT

Holly Waterfield pressed her foot on the gas and hoped to God Hayden and Sarah weren't on to her.

She'd driven away. Accelerated away from Hayden. Left him behind in the middle of that mass of infected, that pile of zombies. A flash. A momentary flash in her mind that told her now was her opportunity. Her opportunity to get Hayden out of the way. Her opportunity to increase her odds of reaching Holyhead successfully.

Because she didn't want to kill Hayden. No, of course she didn't want to kill Hayden. She didn't want to kill anybody.

But nobody could know the truth.

The truth about the bite.

The truth about Holyhead.

If they found out, they'd kill her.

So it was only fair. It was only fair really.

She glanced in the mirror. Saw Hayden and Sarah sitting in the back seat. Both of them staring into the mirror at Holly. Suspicion in their eyes. It was justified. Sarah had been in the car when Holly drove off, after all. And she'd shouted at her. Screamed at her to go back. To return for Hayden.

And Holly came so close.

She came so close to turning around and firing a bullet between Sarah's eyes.

To finishing her.

And powering on to Holyhead.

But she couldn't. Something had stopped her. Moral duty, some bullshit like that. A responsibility. Because she'd seen how much Sarah and Hayden trusted her. Well, maybe not trusted, but how much faith they placed in her anyway. She'd seen that, and she valued that. It was important. Something she couldn't ignore.

She wanted to ignore it, but she couldn't.

Not yet.

Eventually—sometime very soon—she'd have to.

Holly drove past more abandoned cars. Past more boarded up buildings, words like *GOD SAVE US* and *REPENT FUCKING REPENT* scrawled in red across windows. Words that Holly was used to seeing. Horrors that she was accustomed to wherever she travelled, wherever her journey took her.

She hoped God would save her.

And she hoped, in time, that she'd be able to repent for her sins.

Not the sins she'd already committed. They were in abundance. But the sins she was about to commit.

"Thank you."

The voice came from the back seat. Drifted through into Holly's consciousness. Unexpected, soft.

Holly looked in the mirror and saw Hayden looking at her. Blood and sweat crusting on his forehead. Shirt torn from his body.

Holly cleared her throat. Attempted a smile. Tried to keep everything cool, everything in order. "It's—"

"You shouldn't have come back for me. Neither of you. It … it was dangerous. What you did. Suicide. But we're here. So thank you."

He looked right into Holly's eyes and Holly couldn't help but stay focused on them, couldn't help absorb the burning sensation they lit up in her body.

He was thankful.

He was grateful.

He was right where Holly needed him to be.

She caught a glance of Sarah as she went to focus on the debris-laden road ahead. Caught a glance of her looking into the mirror, but not with the same warmth as Hayden. Not with the same naive understanding. With distrust. The same distrust she'd always had.

But that was okay.

Sarah wouldn't be around much longer anyway.

Not with the crushed painkillers Holly had been sneaking into her water ever since they'd set off.

Not with the pale look on her face. The blood dribbling down her nose. The saliva drooling down her chin.

So Holly just smiled back at her.

Smiled at her, then looked at the road ahead.

Maybe Sarah was infected. Maybe the infection was airborne.

But maybe she wasn't. Didn't really matter either way. She'd be dead soon anyway.

And then, Hayden would follow.

One way or another, Hayden would follow.

But for now, Holly just kept her focus on the widening road ahead.

On the barren drive to Holyhead.

And she thought of the best and most effective ways to get rid of Hayden and Sarah.

TWENTY-NINE

Hayden watched Sarah grow even paler as she lifted the murky bottle of water to her lips.

Rain lashed down on the windscreen. Sounded like zombie claws scratching against the glass, against the paintwork. And although Holyhead was approaching, although they were getting closer and closer to some kind of answers, some kind of freedom, Hayden couldn't help but shake the unavoidable feeling of dread deep in the pit of his stomach.

Sarah's pale, sweaty face. Her bloodshot eyes. Snot drooling in a constant bloody stream out of both nostrils.

She was sick. Very sick, as she sipped at the remains of her final bottle of water, the one bottle she'd held on to. The one Hayden insisted he didn't want to sip, as did Holly. Not because of a fear of catching an infection. But simply because Sarah needed it more than him. She needed to stay hydrated. She needed to stay strong.

Well, *staying* strong was perhaps the wrong way to put it. She needed strength, pure and simple.

"What d'you actually think they'll do to me when we get there?" Sarah asked.

Hayden turned. Looked at her. Beyond her, through the back window of the car, rainfall distorted the view. Impossible to see beyond. To see what lurked. What awaited. What watched them.

"They'll be able to help," Hayden said.

"And you know that?" Sarah asked, sniffing. "You—you know that for sure?"

Hayden swallowed a lump in his throat. He couldn't lie. He couldn't pretend he knew exactly what lay ahead for Sarah, for any of them. And there was nothing kind about reassurance. It was cruel if anything. 'Cause that just meant that if everything got snatched away, it'd hurt a hell of a lot more.

"We can't pretend to know what's ahead. None of us. But we're in this together. One way or another we're in this together."

Sarah nodded. Shivery. So shivery her teeth were chattering.

Hayden looked into the front mirror of the car. Caught Holly glancing back at them. That same tearful look in her eyes. That uncertain look.

And then he remembered she'd come back for him. She'd stood with him, stood with Sarah, so everything was good. Everything was okay.

They were making it to Holyhead.

"Sometimes I ... I think I've been selfish," Sarah said.

"Selfish how?"

"I—When I started feeling ill. Before then, even. When—when we saw the message. The message about the infection being airborne. I shouldn't have come. Should've stayed behind. Shouldn't—shouldn't have put any of you at risk."

Hayden saw the sadness in Sarah's eyes. Saw the fear on her gaunt, starving face.

Then he reached for her hand. It was boiling. Absolutely boiling hot.

"You just drink your water," he said. "We're here with you. That's all that matters. We're here with you and we're going to make this. Not gonna let anything happen to you. Or to anyone."

Sarah looked back at Hayden. Slight glassiness to her eyes.

Then she forced the best smile she could and lifted the water bottle to her lips.

In the rear-view mirror, Hayden caught Holly looking back once more.

"You okay?" Hayden asked.

Holly looked away. Then looked back, quivery smile on her face. "I—I should be the one thanking you. For bringing me along. Even though … even though I'm bit. I should be thanking both of you."

Hayden leaned forward. Looked through the window, the snapped wipers slashing away what they could of the rain. Nothing but open road. Holyhead approaching. Fate approaching.

"You came back for me. You're the one I should be—"

"No," Holly said. And she raised her voice in a way Hayden hadn't heard, never before. "You let me in in the first place. You let me in. You—you came with me. To Holyhead. I owe it to you."

She stopped. Hayden saw her fingers tighten on the steering wheel.

Saw tears building up in her eyes.

"I just wanted to … to thank you. I want you to know that. I want you to know I'm—"

"Need to puke!" Sarah shouted.

Hayden swung around. Saw Sarah's face was a light shade of green. A colour that no human face should ever be.

Her cheeks were stretched like a pufferfish. Her eyes were watering, blood vessels burst in them.

"Stop the car," Hayden said.

Holly kept her foot on the gas. "Hayden, I—"

"Just stop the car right this second."

She didn't. Not for a moment. She kept on driving. Sarah kept on heaving. Her cheeks stretching even wider.

"Stop the—"

The car slammed to a halt.

The engine stopped.

Rain bulleted down on the roof.

Sarah scrambled for the handle. Grabbed it, pushed it open, rushed across the dusty ground into the grassy verge and fell to her knees.

She let out her guts. Let out all the contents of her guts.

And Hayden thought about staying put. Thought about staying inside the car until he saw the blood laced vomit spilling out of Sarah's mouth.

Until he saw the movement in the grass up ahead.

Heard the groan.

"Sarah!"

He lunged out of the car. Ran across the road. Ran into the grass, past Sarah, right into the zombie.

Slammed himself shoulder first into its chest.

Sent it flying back into the mud.

Cracked its head on contact with the ground.

He pulled away. Looked down at the zombie beneath him. Bald. Too bald to be healthy. Chemo patient by the looks of things. Still dressed in a blue hospital gown, torn in the middle where it'd been bitten open. Skeletal cheeks. Tarantula fingers.

Groaning and growling and doing everything it could to snap at Hayden.

Hayden felt pity for the zombie as he wrapped his hands around its neck, its skin and flesh soft and bloated.

He felt pity as his fingernails split through the zombie's skin.

Pushed into its neck.

Sliced through its crumbling flesh until it reached the bony tip of its spinal cord.

He felt pity as this zombie scrambled and scrambled, coughed up blood, as he tightened his hands around the bone.

Dragged it upwards.

Hard.

Nothing happened first time. Nothing at all.

The zombie kept on twisting and turning, spitting blood out of its ghastly-smelling mouth at him.

And Hayden kept on pulling.

Kept on pulling even though he saw more shadows and silhouettes in the grass beyond.

Heard more throaty groans.

Kept on pulling as he heard Sarah spew up some more.

Kept on pulling as …

He heard the car door slam shut.

Heard a shout.

Holly's shout.

When he turned around, he didn't see Holly. Didn't see her in the car. Didn't see her outside the car.

The car was empty.

All he saw was the slightest movement in the long grass at the opposite side of the road.

He tried to figure out what'd happened. Tried to figure out if this was some kind of trap. If this was some marauders working against him. Working against all of them.

He looked at the zombie on the ground, all the flesh dragged away from its yellow spinal cord.

Then he looked up at the three, four zombies stumbling through the grass.

He wanted to deal with them. He wanted to put them down.

But he couldn't.

Not right now.

Not while Holly was in danger.

So he stood.

He stood and he slammed his boot down on the zombie's neck, finally heard the deafening crack he'd been waiting for.

Then he ran towards Sarah, still spitting out vomit.

"Come on!" he shouted.

And even though she wasn't ready, even though she was in pain, even though she could barely move, Hayden grabbed her.

Ran past the grass.
Ran in the direction of the movement.
'Cause he wasn't leaving Holly behind.
He wasn't leaving anyone behind.
Even if it cost him his life.

THIRTY

Hayden took his hand away from the car and rushed into the tall grass.

He held onto Sarah. Her body weak, flailing with every step. He kind of wanted to leave her behind. Leave her in the car. But he knew that was way too risky. Too much chance the zombies would surround the car. Too much chance of them smashing through the glass, forcing their way inside, tearing Sarah from the back seat.

He didn't want to bring Sarah along with him on his search for Holly.

But he knew he had no choice.

"Just keep moving," Hayden said, as the tall rain-soaked grass brushed against his bare chest. Sarah clung to his arm, her body growing weaker as the rain lashed down even heavier from the blackening sky. Behind, Hayden heard oncoming zombies. Zombies getting closer. Zombies that wouldn't give up the chase, not for anything.

They were onto him.

They wouldn't stop chasing him.

He just had to accept that, and he had to find Holly.

He scanned the grass. Scanned beyond the grass to the trees. To a wooden fence between the verge and these trees. Whoever took Holly must've taken her down there. Dragged her down there.

But she couldn't have gone far. Not in this weather, not the way running through mud was like skating on an ice rink.

She had to be close.

She couldn't be far away.

Hayden couldn't give up.

Hayden tried to listen beyond the lashing rain, beyond Sarah's throaty gasps, beyond the growls and footsteps of the infected. He tried to listen for a sign of life. A sign of a scream. Some sign that Holly was close—that she was okay—that he could still save her.

But there wasn't a sound.

Not a single sound.

Nothing.

"Hayden!"

Hayden heard Sarah's voice—heard her shout—and he wasn't sure what she was shouting about, not at first.

When he looked to his left, looked where Sarah was looking, he understood.

Zombies. Four zombies flanking from the left.

Running through the grass like lions closing in on their prey.

Hunting.

He turned. Ran to the right. Ran into the taller grass, Sarah still clinging onto him. The grass was so tall. So tall that all visibility ceased; that all he had to go on were the grunts of the zombies, all he had to trust was his faith, his intuition.

His senses.

He ran further through the grass, and all the while the storm raged even louder and heavier above. And the further he ran, the more his faith slipped. Faith in finding Holly. Faith in finding whoever had captured her. Because they were lost.

They were stuck in the tall grass with no visibility and they were lost.

Holly was lost.

Hayden stopped when he heard Sarah heave. He stopped, gave her a moment to spew some more.

More blood.

Thick, red blood.

He looked at Sarah as blood dribbled down her chin. As it stained the grass below. She put her hands on her knees, looked up at him.

"You ... are you—"

"You should—you should go," Sarah said.

Hayden walked over to her. Went to put a hand on her back. "I'm not—"

"No," Sarah said, slapping Hayden's hand away. She looked at him sternly. Looked at him with power. "No. You—you shouldn't touch me. You should leave me."

"I'm not leaving you."

"I'm dying," Sarah said. And although she shouted it, although she screamed it, Hayden heard the fragility in her voice. Saw the emotion building in her eyes.

The acceptance bubbling under the surface.

Behind her, the growls of the zombies got louder.

"I told you I wasn't going anywhere," Hayden said. "That none of us were—"

"You go back to the car," Sarah said. "You—you go back to the car and you get to Holyhead. You get there and you save yourself."

"I'm not prepared to do that, Sarah."

"Then we all die."

Hayden looked up at the sky. Looked up at the thickening clouds. Felt the bitter breeze crash against his topless body.

And he took a deep breath.

"Then so be it," he said.

He walked over to Sarah.

Put a hand out to place on her back.

And this time, even though she tried to slap it away, he forced it onto her back anyway.

Let it rest there.

And faced the shaking grass.

"Hayden what're you—"

"If all of us die out here then so be it. So be fucking it. Because Holyhead isn't worth it. Survival alone isn't fucking worth it if it means ... if it means giving up on the ones you care about."

He stared into the shaking grass.

Listened to the cries, the footsteps, get closer.

"Hayden you know that's not true. You know survival's the most important—"

"I've watched too many people die," Hayden said. Memories of his parents. And his sister.

And Gary ...

"I've ... I've watched too many people fall. And I'm not letting that happen. Not again. I'm not going to—to form a bond with someone else only for it all to fall apart again. No. This is it. If this is where it ends then this is where it ends. So be it. I'm ... I think I'm ready."

He looked into Sarah's eyes.

Sarah looked back at him, bloodshot eyes glistening.

"Thank you," he said, as the footsteps approached.

"For what?"

He felt himself smiling. "For always being you."

He pulled her close.

Closed his eyes as the zombies' cries came within metres.

And then ...

He heard it.

Heard it split through the gasps, through the wind and through the rain like a battering ram in intensity.

The sound of an engine.

An engine starting up.

Tyres screeching against tarmac.

Smell of fumes filling the air.

Hayden and Sarah looked at one another. Both with a familiar disbelief. Both with a familiar confusion.

But deep down, Hayden saw it in Sarah's eyes. Saw his own feelings reflected.

A realisation.

Neither of them had to speak a word after that.

They just ran to their left.

Ran through the grass.

Zombies so close they could feel their jaws snapping inches behind.

They ran through the mud as the engine revved.

They clambered through the grass as more fumes filled the air.

And when they reached the top of the hill, the side of the road, they understood.

When they saw the Honda Civic departing, both of them understood.

"It's ... it's gone," Sarah said, hanging onto Hayden's arm.

And as the zombies got closer behind, Hayden could only watch the car disappear down the road. The road now scattered with zombies. The road to Holyhead, suddenly longer and more dangerous now they were on foot.

All he could do was watch the car drive away.

Stare through the back window at the silhouette in the driver's seat.

Stare at Holly, her eyes looking back at him through the rear-view mirror.

Then, gone.

THIRTY-ONE

"What now?" Sarah asked.

The words resonated in Hayden's mind as he walked as fast as he could down the derelict A-Road. Every now and then, a rusty sign marking Holyhead. But the distance never seemed to get any closer. Forty miles. Thirty-eight miles. Thirty-six miles.

And Hayden was exhausted. Sarah was exhausted.

Not just physically, but mentally.

After Holly's departure.

Holly's betrayal.

"Maybe she didn't—" Sarah started.

"She did," Hayden said. He rubbed his fingers around the metal cap in his pocket. Felt its cool, smooth surface as he stared on down the cloudy road. Quiet. Empty. No sign of life—or dead—for quite some time.

Which was good. For now. While it lasted.

Because it never lasted. It never would.

"I just—I just don't get why—"

"She lied to us," Hayden said, his legs like jelly. "I ... I don't want to accept she did, but she did. For whatever reason, she lied to us."

"About Holyhead?"

"I don't know. That's why we have to keep moving. That's why we have to find out."

They walked further down the middle of the road. Hayden's mouth was as dry as sandpaper. He turned and looked at Sarah. Saw a bit of colour returning to her cheeks, the whiteness peeking from behind the burst blood vessels in her eyes. "How you feeling?"

Sarah sniffed. Nodded. "Better."

"Where's your water?"

She pointed over her shoulder, back in the direction of the spot where Holly abandoned them. "Dropped it back there. Felt a lot better since, weirdly."

And then she stopped.

Stared ahead.

"Sarah?"

Hayden walked up to her. Saw her looking at something. Something down the road.

But when he turned, there was nothing there.

Nothing but cracked concrete. Crows perched on the edge of battered traffic lights. Blood smeared across the pavement, leading right up to the steps of a flat.

The smear of blood ending at the pram.

"Sarah, it's—"

"The water," Sarah said. "The—the water. I ... I've felt better. Since the water."

"You're not making sense."

She looked at Hayden. Looked right into his eyes. "Holly. Back at—back when we set off. She—she gave me her water. She gave me it. And ... and since then I—"

"What're you getting at?"

Sarah paused. Paused to take a breath. Silence filled the road.

"I think she might've been poisoning me," Sarah said.

Hayden couldn't understand Sarah's words. Not at first. He couldn't comprehend the implications.

"Sarah, that's … that's not—"

"I remember thinking. I remember thinking it tasted—tasted off. Right from the start."

"I think you're being paranoid."

"I think you're being blind," she said.

And Hayden understood exactly what she meant right away.

Even though he walked, even though Sarah walked with him, he couldn't feel his body.

He'd trusted Holly. He'd been the one to let her in.

And she'd been the one to betray that trust.

"That bitch," Sarah said, tears streaming down her face. "That fucking bitch."

"We still don't know. For sure."

"I know she—"

"But if she did it means you're … you're not infected."

Hayden saw a momentary light in Sarah's eyes. A sudden flash of realisation, of understanding.

But then that faded.

Faded in an instant.

"I nearly died," she said. "I—I might still die."

Hayden walked up to her.

Took her hand, boiling hot but shivering.

"I'm not going to let that happen," he said. "Now come on. We're going to get some answers."

They walked further down the endless road. It was painfully silent. Torturously empty. Wouldn't believe that the presence of zombies could actually be a good thing until you experienced it for yourself. At least when you could see them, you knew they were there. You knew where you stood.

On this road, abandoned cars. Broken down cars. Smashed windows. Blood-soaked concrete.

And silence.

"I don't know how you can be so sure," Sarah said.

"About what?"

"About us making it to Holyhead. About 'getting answers.'"

Hayden moved the cap around in his pocket. Wasn't sure he was even following the right road, but it was the best road to Holyhead. Holly had been pretty insistent of that. Unless that was just a trick too. Unless that was just another part of her plan.

Whatever. They had to push on to Holyhead.

"Whatever Holly lied about, there's something in Holyhead. Some reason she's heading there."

"Because she's fucking crackers?" Sarah said.

Hayden stared ahead. Felt raindrops dripping down his still-bare chest. "There has to be a reason."

He felt the cap between his fingers again when he saw the movement up ahead.

His first instinct was to reach for the wrench in his pocket. To go ahead and attack the zombie before it reached him—before it reached Sarah.

But then he looked a little closer.

Saw the Honda Civic.

Saw the source of the movement.

So his muscles loosened.

He raised a finger. Pointed up the road.

"There," he said.

Sarah started to say something but Hayden didn't hear her.

He was already walking down the middle of the road.

Fast.

Powering towards the source of the movement.

The petrol cap now in hand.

When he reached the Honda Civic, when she turned to look at him, tears streaming down her face as she leaned against the side of the car—a puddle of pungent petrol spilling onto the road—Hayden couldn't say a word.

He could only look at Holly.

Stare at her.

Stare at the guilt in her eyes.

"I'm sorry," Holly said. "I'm—I'm so sorry."

But Hayden still couldn't bring himself to forgive her.

Only to reach into his pocket for the wrench.

Step towards her.

THIRTY-TWO

Hayden lifted the wrench and stormed towards Holly. Everything was a blur. Sarah grabbing his arm. Pulling it back. Holly with tears running down her face as she leaned against the broken-down Honda Civic, the same Civic Hayden had removed the leaky petrol cap from when he'd first seen Holly disappear. Mainly because he worried about someone taking it. Of what they might do.

But also because he worried about Holly taking it.

A small, niggling part inside asking the question: can you trust her? Should you trust her?

And as it turned out, the answer was a resounding "no".

"You could've killed us," Hayden said, lifting the wrench higher, moving closer to Holly.

"Hayden—" Sarah said.

Hayden pushed her back. "You could've killed us. You—you fucking left us for dead."

"I didn't mean for it to turn out this way," Holly said. Her voice sounded worn out. Exhausted, even. She didn't look like she had any fight left in her.

"Then how the fuck did you mean it to turn out, hmm?"

Hayden asked, doing all he could not to crack Holly's skull for her betrayal. "How the fuck was this supposed to end?"

"Just—just—"

"What aren't you fucking telling us—"

"There's no safe place in Holyhead!"

The words cut through Hayden's consciousness like a chainsaw through wood. They echoed down the silent dual-carriageway. Words he'd suspected. Words he'd *expected*, even.

But words he didn't want to hear.

Because hearing them meant making it this far was all for nothing.

Hearing them meant there was no hope. No hope at all.

Hayden lowered the wrench. His heart pounded. He could taste sweat dripping down his lips. "Why lie?"

Holly didn't answer. She just leaned against the car. Head pressed right up to the window. Moving it from side to side. Crying.

"I said why fucking—"

"I needed—I needed to get there," Holly said. "I—Someone I love. My husband. Ex-husband. He's there. He works there. And I just ... I wasn't strong enough. No one's strong enough alone. Please. I'm sorry. I'm so sorry."

Hayden struggled to wrap his head around the harsh reality of the words. Holly just wanted to find her husband—her ex-husband. She needed someone to help her get to Holyhead.

"You used us."

"I know and I'm—"

"You almost got us killed. You ... you got Gary killed."

Holly kept on shaking her head. Kept on sniffing. Rain trickled down from the grey storm clouds above.

"Tell me one thing." Sarah's voice. Hayden had almost forgotten she was here with him. So entranced in the moment. So gripped by rage.

Holly lifted her head and right away Hayden saw guilt in her tear-soaked eyes when she looked at Sarah.

"The water," Sarah said, her voice quivery now. "You ... you spiked it. Didn't you? You spiked it."

Holly's bottom lip shook.

She didn't shake her head.

Didn't protest.

She didn't have to.

"You evil fucking bitch," Sarah said. But there was a fragment of relief to her voice too. Relief at the fact that she wasn't infected. She hadn't caught the virus after all. "You ... you selfish fucking—"

"I never wanted to hurt you," Holly said.

"How can you say that?" Sarah shouted. "How—how can you possibly fucking say you never wanted to hurt us when you—when you tried to kill me? When you left us both for dead?"

Holly didn't have an answer to that.

All she could do was shake her head.

"I'm sorry. I'm sorry."

Hayden's mind raced. Raced with all kinds of thoughts, all sorts of theories. Things Holly had told him. Truths and half-truths he'd believed.

"The bite," Hayden said. "The bite. On your arm. The story about ... about surviving. Surviving a bite. Not getting infected."

He didn't want to ask the question.

He didn't want to know the truth.

But he had to.

The look on Holly's face didn't change.

She didn't say a word, not right away.

And that was enough for Hayden to know.

The bite mark was a lie.

"I ... I was with another group," Holly said. "And bad things, bad things happened to them. So I ... I moved on. I moved on but I was so scared. I needed—I needed something that made me extraordinary. Something that—that made me more than just an ordinary woman. I needed …"

She looked down at the bandage around her arm.

She didn't have to say any more.

Hayden couldn't speak. Not for a moment. And while he was angry, there was another prevailing feeling inside. The feeling of intense grief. The death of hope. Holly had been a beacon of light in a dark, violent world. She'd been an end goal. She'd been extraordinary, just like she said.

But she wasn't.

She was just normal.

A normal girl who'd dragged them miles across the country in hope of finding her ex-husband.

"Why lie?" Hayden asked.

"What?"

"Why lie to us? About all this? Why lie?"

Holly wiped her eyes. Stepped away from the car. "If I'd told you the truth, would you have helped me make it this far?"

Hayden didn't answer.

Figured he didn't need to.

They stood there in the wind. Rain falling down heavier. In the distance, right up the road in the direction of Holyhead, the silhouettes of zombies. Zombies drifting towards them. Edging closer. Far enough away for them not to pose a threat right now, but on their way. Like they always were. Like they always would be.

"I know what I did was bad—"

"Bad?" Sarah shouted. She sat on the concrete shaking her head. Colour had returned to her cheeks in abundance. Red. Angry red.

"I—I can only say I'm sorry. But—but I was desperate. I needed someone. And … and all I can say is I'm sorry. Please."

Hayden walked over to the Honda Civic.

Opened the boot, pulled out a rubber pipe from inside.

Stuck it in the petrol tank, then walked over to a white Seniors coach, stuck the other end in its fuel tank.

Let the petrol trickle from the higher tank of the coach into the Honda Civic.

Not lots, but enough.

Enough to get them to more petrol.

Enough to get them away from here.

Nobody said a word while Hayden filled the Civic's tank. Just watched the shadows of the mass of zombies drift closer. Heard their echoing groans pick up in volume, in intensity.

When he'd drained the coach of all the juice he could, he took the pipe away, shoved it in the Civic's boot and slipped the petrol cap back on the tank.

He walked up to Holly. His wrench still tight in his sweaty palms. Heart still racing. So many things he wanted to say to her. So many things he wanted to do to her, to punish her.

He took a deep breath in through his nostrils.

"You did what you had to do to get this far," Hayden said.

And then he opened the car door.

Waved at Sarah to get inside.

"But this is as far as you go," he said.

He climbed in through the passenger seat and clipped his belt on while Sarah started the engine.

"Wait," Holly said, slapping her palms against the windscreen. The tears flowing again. "Please. I—I'm sorry. Don't leave me out here. Don't—"

"I wouldn't shout too loud," Hayden said, as Sarah turned the car around, back in the direction of Riversford, back in the direction of their home. "The zombies'll be on to you in a few minutes. I think now's a good chance to run."

He nodded at Sarah.

Sarah put her foot down.

Accelerated back down the derelict dual-carriageway.

As they moved, Hayden heard Holly crying. Heard her shouting, screaming at him to come back.

Saw her in the wing mirror. Saw her and the shadows of the zombies behind her, getting closer to her, closer and closer.

Above her, the sign to Holyhead. The sign to the false beacon of hope. The place they'd trusted in, believed in, given everything up to get to, gone.

"You okay?" Sarah asked.

Hayden stared at Holly in the cracked wing mirror as she got smaller and smaller, smaller and smaller, until she was gone.

"I am now," he said.

But he wasn't.

He really wasn't.

THIRTY-THREE

Holly stared at the oncoming mass of zombies and wondered how the hell she'd fucked up so much to end up in this position.

They were beautiful, in a way. The infected. The way they moved so uniformly, like towels drying on a washing line in the wind. She thought back to her old house on Cranston Drive. First place her and Andy had bought together. Barely earning enough to pay the mortgage, but fuck, that didn't matter. What mattered was they had a *home*. A place they could call theirs. A proper place with a nice kitchen and a double bed and a cosy lounge and, yes, a washing line.

A washing line, even though it always rained. Always frigging rained.

But it was home.

And it was lovely.

And then Andy met someone better than her and it was gone, he was gone.

She listened to the echoing cries of the zombies, the cold wind creeping through her shirt, tingling her already icy skin. She wasn't afraid. Wasn't afraid to look them in the eyes, look her own fate in the eyes. Not anymore. Because she'd got what she deserved. She'd done a terrible thing—no, done terrible *things*—and she was being punished for her mistakes. It was only right that she paid for her mistakes.

She owed it to Sarah.

To Hayden.

To all the people who'd fallen because of her—fallen trying to help her, protect her, look out for her because they felt she was important—she owed it to them.

She licked her dried, chapped lips and wished she had some water. Water. What she'd done to Sarah's water. Tampered with it. Made her sick. That was an awful thing to do. Something she'd done early, something she regretted the more she got to know Hayden and Sarah, the more she learned about them, the more she saw them as people. Not just taxis, not just a vessel to get her to Holyhead, to get her to Andy, but *people*.

She'd crossed a line when she'd given Sarah the pill-filled drink. She knew that. Knew it was something she'd never be able to get away with—that she'd never forgive herself for.

She'd made a mistake.

She'd made so many mistakes in the name of reaching her ex-husband.

In the name of standing by his side once again.

In the name of love.

Hadn't everyone made a mistake in the name of love at some point in their lives?

Holly looked over her shoulder. Looked down the road where Hayden and Sarah had driven. She couldn't blame them for turning away. Couldn't knock them for turning their back on Holyhead. Sure, her story about Holyhead was lightweight in the first place, but one thing she'd learned in her time in this new world was that people would go to crazy extents in the name of one small thing: hope.

She'd given Hayden hope. She'd given Sarah hope.

Now she was paying the price for tearing that hope away.

It was only right.

She turned back around and looked in the middle of the mass of zombies. Got herself ready to set off. To walk. To find another way to Holyhead. Because she couldn't give up. She had to keep on going. Had to keep on fighting, right to the bitter end.

When she looked down the road, she saw something.

Something different. Something in the middle of the zombies. Something that wasn't there, not before. Something ...

Her fists tightened.

Her mouth opened.

Her heart picked up.

She saw what was ahead.

What was coming towards her.

A silver vehicle. About the size of a coach. Ploughing its way through the zombies. Accelerating right towards her.

Holly swallowed a lump in her throat. Held her breath. Tried to cook up a story. 'Cause these people could help her. They could take her to Holyhead.

But no. They were coming from Holyhead. They were coming from Holyhead so they had to know. Know she was lying.

She had to think of something else.

Something to convince them.

Something to earn their trust.

She tore the bandage away from her "bitten" wrist as the vehicle powered closer, the smell of gasoline rich in the air. Scratched at the healing wound until it bled again, looked fresh. She tore away some of her shirt. Made herself look broken, lost. Like she'd been in a car accident. Or like she'd been walking out here for days. Walking for days, narrowly surviving, and ...

The vehicle stopped right beside her.

The engine didn't stop, though. So loud, blocking all sense of her surroundings. She looked up at the side door to this coach-like vehicle. A massive coach spray-painted silver, all of the windows blocked up.

Movement in the wing mirror.

Holly started to feel a little uncertainty creep up her body when the passenger door opened.

When a bulky man with long grey hair leaned out and looked down at her. Rotting black teeth. Smell of sweat strong in the air.

"Y'alright, missy?"

Holly moved her arm behind her back. She didn't want to be with these people. She couldn't trust them. She'd find someone else. She'd—

"Hey. I'm talkin' to yer. Rude to ignore. Y'alright?"

Holly lowered her head. Walked towards the back of the coach. She had to run. She had to hide. Whatever she did, she had to get away.

Closer to the back of the coach.

Engine still rumbling.

Not a word from—

Then a hand on her shoulder.

A shitty-tasting hand around her mouth.

Dragging her back towards the coach.

"Rude to ignore," a man said, then licked her cheek with his long, eel-like tongue.

Holly struggled. Struggled as piss crept down her thigh. Struggled and struggled to get his hand away, to tell them, tell them anything so they'd let her go, let her free.

"I—I'm bitten," she shouted, still struggling, still kicking and fighting. "I'm—I'm bitten."

The man behind her stopped dragging her. Stood still. She could feel his heavy heart racing. Smell the booze on his breath, in his hair.

He loosened his grip on Holly and Holly prepared to run. Prepared to leg it away from here. Anyone but this man. Anywhere but here.

And as she moved, she felt his hand tighten again.

Felt him drag her back.

Grab her mouth.

Press his lips to her right ear.

"I don't give a shit whether you been bit or not," he said.

And then, as much as Holly struggled, fought, kicked and spat, the man dragged her back to the passenger door of the coach.

Dragged her up the steps.

Dragged her into his lair.

Slammed the door shut.

He pushed her down into a damp seat. The smell of sweat strong in the air. Sweat and blood. Sweat and rot.

Flies buzzing all over the place.

Maggots dripping from the ceiling.

"Buckle up," the man said, dragging Holly's wrists around the back of the first chair and cuffing them tight behind it. "Gonna be one helluva ride."

He spun the loose, broken chair around so Holly could see the back of the coach.

Holly thought she was afraid. She thought she knew what it was to be terrified.

But when she looked into the back of this coach, she really did understand.

For the first time in her life, she felt pure terror.

THIRTY-FOUR

Hayden wasn't sure how long Sarah had been driving.

Only that the road didn't change. The abandoned cars he'd got so sick of seeing didn't change. The bodies he'd grown so accustomed to piled up. Men. Women. Children. Animals.

All of them had ignited nausea inside him whenever he used to see them.

Now they were just a part of the backdrop. A part of the surroundings. Like trees.

Like abandoned cars.

Like zombies.

"Guessing we'll just head back then," Sarah said.

It wasn't really a question. More a fact. After all, what else was there to do but head back to Riversford?

"Least we'll see Martha and Amy again," Sarah continued, her foot right down on the accelerator. Hayden didn't want to look at the fuel gauge. Didn't want to know how much or how little petrol they had left. Cross that bridge when they came to it.

All that mattered now was ...

What mattered now?

What mattered at all anymore?

"Hopefully they're okay. We should never have—"

"You feeling better?" Hayden asked.

Sarah glanced over at him. The colour was back to her cheeks. Her hair was still mangly, but fuck—so was everyone's now. She half-smiled at him. Nodded. "Yeah. Yeah I am. Are you?"

Hayden looked away then. He didn't like people asking him if he was okay, not anymore. Not since the world went to shit. Because he wasn't. He really fucking wasn't. How could anyone be okay? How could anyone even pretend to be okay anymore?

"I'm fine," he said.

Sarah turned back. Looked ahead at the road. In the trees to the right of them, Hayden saw movement. The familiar movement of zombies. Infected stepping out onto the concrete, alerted by the roar of the engine. "What Holly did," she said. "What happened to Gary—"

"I killed Gary," Hayden said.

He wasn't expecting the words to leave his mouth. Wasn't expecting to ever make the confession. But he did. He did and the words were out there, irreversible, hanging in the air like something dead.

Sarah looked at him again. Narrowed her eyes. "What ... what d'you mean you—"

"He stepped in that trap and I ... I couldn't get him out," Hayden said, the flow of words failing to cease. "I tried. I tried but—but the zombies were so close. They were so close to both of us—"

"Hayden, slow down. What are you saying?"

"I knocked him out then I left a saw by his side and I ..." He tasted vomit. Gulped it down, burning his throat. "I left him for dead."

There was a silence in the car then. A long, drawn out silence that seemed to grow more uncomfortable the more time stretched on. And Hayden understood why. He understood his own hypocrisy. The hypocrisy of leaving Holly to fend for herself all because she'd been selfish. The same level of selfishness he'd shown, only on a different level.

'Cause everyone was selfish in this world. That was the truth. Everyone had to be selfish to survive.

"Did you ... did you have no choice?" Sarah asked.

"I had a choice," Hayden said. "There's—there's always a choice."

"Would you have died if—"

"I knocked him out 'cause I didn't want him to suffer. I—I left the saw by his side just in case. But there was no way he was coming out of that trap without both of us dying. There was no way he was—"

"Then you did the right thing," Sarah said.

She looked at Hayden. Nodded. And Hayden saw a flicker of detachment in her eyes. A look of, "I'd do the same to you."

He hoped that wasn't the case.

Hoped it wasn't true.

But everyone had to do what they had to, to survive.

Everyone had to be selfish.

That was just the way of the world now.

"I didn't do the right thing," Hayden said.

"Hayden you—"

"I did the only thing. Sometimes the only thing isn't the right thing."

He thought back to Holly.

Thought back to the way he'd left her on the road. Pretty much signed her death sentence. Sure, she'd lied. Sure, she'd tried to fucking kill Sarah.

But she'd done what she thought was the only thing.

She'd done what she thought was the only thing she could to survive.

"Stop the car," Hayden said.

Sarah scanned her surroundings. Instinctive search for infected. "What's up?"

"Stop the car. Turn around."

She turned. Frowned. "Hayden what—"

"We're going back."

"Back where?"

"We're going back for Holly."

Sarah didn't stop the car. She didn't turn it around. "Are you fucking insane? She tried to—"

"I know what she tried to do. I know fucking well what she tried to do. But she only did what we'd do if we thought it might get us to a place we care about most."

"I can't believe you'd actually say that."

"It's the truth," Hayden said, hands tingling. "All of us are selfish. We're fucking driven by our own selfish desires, our own impulses. But that doesn't mean we can't be together. That doesn't mean we're beyond saving."

Sarah shook her head but Hayden could see he'd got through to her. He could see she got what he was saying. They were all gigantic hypocrites in a world of hypocrisy.

But they were all bound by one thing.

The fact that they were human.

"Turn around Sarah. Please."

"She tried to murder me."

"But she didn't murder you. You're still here."

Sarah turned. Looked at Hayden with an expression he couldn't decipher. Either she was going to scream at him or tear his head off, one or the other.

In the end, she did neither.

She took her foot off the gas.

Slowed the car.

Turned the steering wheel.

For a moment, as they spun round and faced the road to Holyhead, Hayden felt apprehension build up inside. Not a bad kind of apprehension. But the apprehension that rose before doing something good. Doing something right.

Holly had tried to kill them.

She'd led them here for her own selfish interests.

But she was human.

She was human and she was sorry and for that reason, she didn't deserve to be left behind.

He had these thoughts for a moment.

And then he saw the towering metal vehicle slamming through the distant zombies and tearing in his direction.

Fast.

THIRTY-FIVE

"You see who's driving?" Sarah asked.

Hayden shook his head. "Not yet. But whoever it is wants to get somewhere in a hurry."

Hayden crouched down under an old red Renault Clio. Stunk of petrol under here, and it was a heck of a tight squeeze.

But it kept them out of the line of sight. Kept them under cover. For now, anyway.

Just had to hope it kept them under cover till the nutter in the silver coach flew past.

And just had to hope the nutter didn't crash into them.

The way they were driving right now, Hayden couldn't be too optimistic.

"Don't like the look of 'em whoever it is," Sarah said.

"Just got to keep our heads low and we'll be okay. Then we'll push back for Holly."

Hayden heard Sarah grimace. Quite audibly.

But she didn't protest.

Instead, she just stated the obvious truth: "If this wackjob leaves us a car to disappear in."

Hayden held his breath as the coach powered closer. On the

front of it, right on the grill, Hayden saw remains. Body parts. Bloodied pieces of flesh—decaying chunks of zombies torn away on its assault down the road. And the louder the tyres screeched against the tarmac, a sense of worry grew inside Hayden. Concern that somewhere down the road, Holly would've bumped into this driver. That they'd knocked her over.

Or worse.

That they'd picked her up.

He just had to hope his paranoia was off the mark, just this once.

The coach flew closer and it didn't seem to slow down. The smell of diesel fumes spewing out of it was strong, and Hayden could feel the heat from its engine even from this distance.

"I ... I don't think it's slowing down," Sarah said.

Hayden stared into the murky window of the oncoming coach. He just had to hope. Hope it'd slow down. Hope it'd spin around the car they were inside. Hope the driver would take a peek inside the Honda Civic if that's what it took to get him to stop.

Just had to hope they'd spin around the vehicle.

Just had to hope they wouldn't have to flee from under this car.

Just had to ...

A squeak. The squeaking of tyres against the concrete. Steam kicking up from them. Diesel fumes getting stronger, so strong they made Hayden's eyes water.

And then the coach ground to a halt.

Ground to a halt right in front of Hayden. Right in front of Sarah.

Right in the middle of the road.

Hayden's heart pounded. He could feel Sarah's pulse racing through the tips of her fingers, too.

He squeezed the end of them.

She squeezed back.

Together, they waited. Hoped.

Nobody got out of the coach. And as much as Hayden tried to arch his neck without giving away any small signs of movement, he couldn't see anyone through the window either. Too dusty. Too dirty.

The engine of the coach kept on rumbling. Behind it, way in the distance, zombies kept on walking. Hayden wanted to look over his shoulder. Wanted to check the other side of the Clio. Got the unwavering sense that he was being watched. That someone was eyeing him up as their prey.

Either a zombie or the person behind the glass.

Movement.

A door creaking open.

The side door of the coach.

The first thing Hayden saw were the leather boots. They made their way down the ladder by the coach entrance. Each step echoing down the empty road.

And then a voice.

A man's voice. Hard to tell what he was saying. Impossible, in fact. But this was a man. This was a man and he was speaking to someone. He was …

He hopped down from the side of the vehicle.

Landed on the road.

He was big. A big, bulky man with long, straggly grey hair and impossibly yellow teeth. He had chains around his neck, a thick leather jacket. His black trousers were torn in places. On his face, a big smile, not at anyone in particular. Just the sign of a man who was totally content with life.

Anyone who was totally content with this life was a cause for concern.

"Well, well, fuckin' lovely day," the man mumbled.

He walked out onto the concrete. Walked in Hayden and Sarah's direction. Every footstep heavy. Solid.

Hayden tightened his grip on Sarah's hand.

"Fuckin' beautiful day to take a break from time to time," he said in this incredibly northern brand of gibberish. Still wasn't clear to Hayden whether the guy was talking to himself or whether he knew damn well he and Sarah were watching him.

Just had to hope.

He didn't want to kill anyone. Not anymore. Didn't want to risk starting a feud with a wider bunch of crazies.

But he would if he had to.

If he absolutely had to.

The man walked right over to the Clio. Slowly. Whistling through the gap in his rotting teeth. The smile still covered his face as he looked up at the sky, scanned the clouds.

"Used to hate days like this," he said. "Used to—to hate it when the clouds came and fuckin' kill-joyed the sun. Not anymore. Not anymore. Beautiful days. Beautiful drivin' days."

He stopped. Stopped right by the bonnet of the Clio.

Hayden let go of Sarah's hand.

Still holding his breath.

He reached for his pocket. Reached for the wrench.

Pulled it out and got ready to swing it.

The man didn't budge. Didn't say another word. All Hayden could see of him were his legs. All he could smell was sweat and piss and shit. Interspersed with cheap aftershave. Like the guy was trying to cover up the fact he reeked but making the stench even more pungent in the process.

"Whaddyoo say, Pamela? Eh? Whaddyoo think?"

Hayden looked around. Looked around for a woman. Someone who might be called Pamela.

But it was just him. Just him alone. Just a lone psycho and a coach.

He could handle someone if they were alone.

He could pull back this wrench and crack his shins and …

The guy unzipped his flies and an immense smell of urine seeped out almost as quickly as the piss itself. The guy peed all over the front of the Clio. Let his dark orange piss seep right down the bonnet, pool on the road in front of them, drift back and cover Hayden and Sarah in its acidic dampness.

The guy just whistled as he kept on pissing, kept on pissing.

When he finally stopped about thirty seconds later, Hayden was holding his breath and doing his best not to puke. His hands and knees were soaked. He could taste the guy's piss on his lips. Couldn't be healthy. Couldn't possibly be healthy.

"Nice day," he said, zipping his flies and scratching his ass. "Nice day. But everyone's just gotta keep on movin' now."

He turned around and walked back towards the coach.

Hayden's stomach started to loosen. His breathing returned, even though the simple act of breathing was nigh on impossible with the stench of piss so strong.

He put his wrench back in his pocket. Grabbed Sarah's hand again.

Waited as the guy climbed up the ladders.

As he pulled the coach door right back.

As he ...

Then Hayden saw it.

He didn't understand at first. Didn't understand what he was looking at. *Who* he was looking at.

And then, in an instant, it clicked.

Holly.

Holly was in that coach.

Tied up in a seat just behind the driver's one.

Gag wrapped around her mouth.

Shaking. Struggling. Crying.

Sarah gasped when she saw her.

She gasped, covered her mouth right away, realising her error.

The guy stopped. Stopped climbing the ladder. Peeked out onto the road.

He looked around, the smile gone from his face. Reached into his baggy pocket and pulled out a knife. Swung it around as he turned, like this was all some big performance to him.

Behind the coach, the zombies got closer.

So close Hayden could hear their footsteps.

"Come on, Pamela," he said, lowering his knife. "Let's get back on the road. Don't wanna be late for supper."

He slammed the coach door shut.

A few seconds later, the coach started moving again.

And as it departed, as it drove around the Clio, around the Civic, Hayden couldn't help but shake the image of Holly tied up in that chair from his mind.

"What now?" Sarah said.

Hayden stared into the mass of oncoming zombies, listened to the tyres of the coach screech against the concrete.

"I think we both know what now," he said.

THIRTY-SIX

When Holly saw what was at the back of the coach, she threw up.

She couldn't control it. Couldn't control her body's reaction to the sight opposite her. The smell. The sounds.

She kept on throwing up even as the man wrapped the gag around her mouth.

Even when he climbed out of the coach.

Even when he got back inside, started up the coach, got them moving again.

Her eyes watered as she thought about what she'd seen when the man turned her around, when he showed her what was at the back of the coach.

The memories as strong and as vivid as reality itself.

The faces. The faces of the women, mouths ripped open right up to their ears.

The flies crawling around them, rubbing their hands as they moved from dead person to dead person.

And then there was their guts. The way each of them held onto their guts. Rested their disembowelled intestines on their laps like they were their children, their beloved.

The stench of shit.

The stench of death.

But most of all it was their faces that stuck with Holly, as this psychopath powered down the road, crashed through more abandoned cars, through more zombies.

It was the look on their faces that got to Holly the most.

Because their eyes looked so alive.

Like they'd died in complete fear. Complete agony.

Like they'd been completely aware of what was happening to them.

Holly listened to the man whistling away. Saw his silhouette in the driver's seat in front of her. She wanted to get away. She had to get away. But her hands were tied behind the back of the seat. Her mouth was gagged, the taste of her own vomit drifting back into her throat. She was stuck. She was trapped.

Just like the other women in the other coach seats.

The coach trip to hell.

"Hell, I can't get over how damned beautiful today really is," the driver shouted. "How 'bout you my Pamela? Can you get over how damned beautiful today really is?"

Holly closed her eyes. They stung from her tears. She squeezed them shut, desperate not to make eye contact with the driver, eager for him not to see. She hoped—prayed—that when she opened her eyes, she'd be back to normality. That she'd be back with Hayden and Sarah and Gary. That she'd be back with them *before* they found out what she'd done. Or that she hadn't done a thing at all. That it'd all just been a figment of her imagination. A dark dream. A sickening hallucination.

But she didn't have to open her eyes to know her prayers fell on deaf ears.

She didn't have to open her eyes 'cause she could still hear the flies buzzing around, still smell rotting, still taste vomit, still feel the cuffs tight around her wrists.

She wanted right then to beg. To beg this man to let her go, as the coach continued to speed down the road. But she knew begging was both fickle and impossible. She'd ended up here because of her own actions. Because of what she'd done to Hayden, to Sarah. Because of the bullshit journey she'd taken them on.

So she didn't beg. She didn't even think about begging.

Instead, she just thought about Andy. Just thought about the warmth of Andy's arms, the way he'd twirl her hair when they lay in bed together. The way he'd look at her with that smile.

She thought about Andy and she hoped to God he still felt the same way about her as she did about him.

Even though he'd moved on, Holly prayed there was still something there.

Maybe there was something there. Maybe there wasn't.

It suddenly didn't matter.

Because Holly heard something behind her.

She opened her eyes. Saw the man looking at the reflection of his rear-view mirror.

"Aw, shit," he said, chuckling.

The movement continued behind Holly.

Shuffling.

Footsteps.

She tried to turn, tried to see what was behind her, but she couldn't. All she knew was something was coming towards her. She'd sworn they were alone. Sworn it was just her and this psycho in here together.

But the footsteps got louder.

And then …

A groan.

The driver chuckled some more. A chuckle that developed into a hearty cough. "Aw, how damned rude of me not to introduce her," he said.

Introduce her.

Footsteps getting louder.

Groans getting closer.

"Dear, meet my Pamela," the driver said.

Movement in the corner of Holly's left eye.

Pamela. But Pamela was supposed to be made up. Pamela was just something he said. Pamela was ...

Someone walking around her side.

Footsteps squelching wet with blood.

"And Pamela, meet my new lovely," he said.

Holly looked into the eyes of the zombie.

Looked into the eyes of the little girl.

And then the little girl opened her mouth and moved towards her neck.

THIRTY-SEVEN

"Are you sure about this, Hayden?"

"No. But I don't see what else we can—"

"We can make him stop."

"Make him stop? How we gonna make him stop?"

"We—we can try and—"

"Just put your foot down," Hayden said. "I've got this."

Sarah pressed her foot harder on the accelerator. "Hope you're right about that."

They hurtled down the road. In the distance, getting closer, the silver coach. The one the babbling psycho had stepped out of—the one whose piss Hayden could still smell in the warmth of this car right now.

They had to get to him.

They had to stop him.

They had to save Holly from whatever fate awaited her.

"He's gonna see us," Sarah said, driving the car.

"Maybe so," Hayden said. He had one hand on the wrench and the other on the passenger door. He knew what he was planning was mad. Insane, even. But sometimes to do the right things—the *real* right things—you had to be willing to do the insane thing to get there.

And anyway, there was no sanity to this world. Not anymore.

Everything crazy was within the realms of normalcy.

"So you're just gonna open your fucking door and jump and—"

"Hope for the best," Hayden said, interrupting Sarah before she could make his plan sound any sillier. He didn't want to dwell on what he was about to do. He just needed to get to the coach. To get onto it somehow.

Then, he had to get Holly out and they had to get away from here.

All of them.

Together.

"You never told me whether you'd rather be buried or cremated," Sarah said.

"Not sure it'll matter if this goes tits up."

"I don't know how you can be so laissez-faire about it all."

"About what all?"

"About death."

Hayden swallowed a lump in his dry throat. Watched the back of the coach get nearer, nearer. "I've spent way too long worrying about death for it to bother me anymore."

"Not sure you'll be saying that if you end up underneath a tyre."

"Maybe not. But let's just hope it doesn't come to that. Now get your foot down."

They sped closer to the rear of the coach. No sign of swerving from the driver. Shit, he looked three sheets to the wind anyway. Hayden had to hope that worked in his favour. In Sarah's favour.

In Holly's favour.

Something told him Holly's odds of survival were somewhat longer than everyone's.

The rear of the coach got closer. So close that the car was almost within touching distance of it. From the trees either side,

Hayden saw zombies walk out. Walk out to see what the fuss was, what the human racket was all about.

But he just stayed focused on the back of the coach.

Just breathed in deeply.

Kept his cool.

"Pull up around the side," Hayden said.

"But won't it be better if—"

"Above the tyre, look," Hayden said, pointing. "Emergency door. I can get in through there."

"And what if there's something waiting for you on the other side?"

Hayden kept on breathing deeply. "Then so be it."

He heard Sarah curse under her breath. Then put her foot even harder on the gas, pull around the side of it.

"She better be worth it to you," Sarah said.

"Holly?"

"She tried to kill me. Tried to kill both of us."

"But she's a survivor. She made it this far. She ... she did what she thought she had to do to survive. She was sorry. So ... so yes. She's worth it to me. Worth it to all of us."

"All of who?"

Hayden watched the rail by the emergency door at the side of the coach get closer. "Humanity."

The Civic was right up beside the coach now. Flying so fast down the motorway that the speed pinned Hayden back into his seat. He looked back. Looked through the rear window. Saw the concrete spinning away under the tyres. Realised how crazy, how insane this plan actually was.

But he knew he had to do it.

Knew he had to try something.

He looked at Sarah. Looked at her as the fear built up in his chest. Fear that he had to control. Fear that he had to keep in check.

He saw the fear in her eyes too.

The sadness.

"If ... if this is it—" Sarah started.

"It won't be," Hayden said. "It won't be it."

He looked at her a few seconds longer. A few seconds that stretched on to what felt like hours. And as he looked into her eyes, he felt something. Felt something spark deep within. Something he'd felt when he first looked into Sarah's eyes. Something that he'd felt all along.

A feeling he wasn't familiar with.

But a feeling he enjoyed.

A feeling he wasn't going to run from. Not anymore.

"I'll find a way," Hayden said, voice quivering with uncertainty. "One ... one way or another I'll find a way."

She half-smiled. "You better do," she said. "You better not leave me on my own out here."

Hayden wanted to turn away. To tell Sarah to pull back from this coach. To back out of saving Holly.

But that was the wrong thing to do.

He didn't leave people behind.

Not anymore.

Not again.

"I'll be back before you know it," Hayden said.

He pulled the handle of the passenger door.

Felt the wind pressing it back, pushing and forcing him to stay put in the car.

"Clarice would be proud," Sarah said.

It was those words that tipped Hayden over the edge. That made emotion well up inside. That awoke a past he tried to forget. A past he distanced himself from.

The last person he'd cared about, the last person he'd loved.

Gone.

But no.

He could love again.

He could make her proud.

He could save Holly. He could get out of here with Sarah. He could—

He thought the wind had just got heavier, stronger, when he felt the pressure slam into the door.

But he knew something was wrong when he felt the car slam to the right.

When his face cracked into the glass.

When everything went red.

And through the redness, Sarah screaming beside him as the car spun, he saw the cause of the damage. Saw the coach veering off the road. Taking the Civic with it.

He wanted to hold Sarah's hand.

Wanted to tell her everything was going to be okay.

But then he felt his head smack against the glass and everything went dark.

The last thing he saw, as the coach came to a stop, was the silhouettes of the zombies approaching in the cracked wing mirror.

And then nothing but darkness.

THIRTY-EIGHT

Hayden tasted blood in his mouth, and he knew he was in trouble.

He tried to move, move from wherever he was but he was trapped. Something was pressing right into his arm. Stabbing into it, even.

The smell of burning was strong in the air. The sound of car alarms, of creaking metal, of ...

Footsteps.

Footsteps and groans.

Hayden turned his head. Blinked the dust from his tender, blurry eyes. It was at that moment he realised he was still strapped into the Honda Civic. The airbag had blown up in his face, but instead of comforting him it was suffocating him.

Through the totally smashed window on his right, he could see the silver coach that Holly was in parked right across the road.

And from behind it, zombies.

"Sarah ..."

Speaking hurt. Hurt his compressed lungs. He tried to shift around; tried to get a view of the driver's seat, a sign that Sarah was alive, that she was okay.

He saw images in his mind as the loose shards of glass and contorted metal dug deeper into his skin. Images of Sarah's head cracked against the windscreen. Of the inside of the car being painted with her blood.

No.

He couldn't accept that.

Sarah couldn't be dead.

She ...

He turned and he saw Sarah.

Saw her with her eyes wide open.

Blood dripping down her forehead.

Staring blankly at Hayden.

The sounds of the zombie footsteps got closer but all Hayden could do was look back into Sarah's eyes. Stare back into those vacant pupils, the light of her life gone, the spark inside absent.

He stared into her eyes and remembered the promise he'd made her—the promise that he wouldn't leave her alone—and he felt his throat tightening up, felt tears building behind his eyelids.

"I'm sorry," he said. "I'm ..."

Then Sarah's eyes moved and she gasped a long breath.

Relief swept through Hayden's body as he watched Sarah move. He couldn't help but smile. Smile, despite the situation they were in. Despite the near-certain death they faced.

"Hayden what ... my leg, it—"

"It's okay," Hayden said. "It's okay."

"My leg hurts so bad."

"I'm here with you. We just—we just need to concentrate right now."

"I'm not sure I can—"

"You can," Hayden said, turning and seeing the zombies edging closer. "You can 'cause you have to. For both of us. Now there's ... the dashboard. I think—I think it's come loose. I can't push it on my own. But if we can shift it a little, I think I can open my door."

Sarah let out a pained gasp as she turned her head to look at the distended dashboard pushing into their chests, squeezing the air out of both of them. "I—I can't—"

A growl. A gasp. Right by the car.

"You have to," Hayden said. "Please. Please don't give up. I promised I'd stay with you and—and if this is the end, then it's the end. But don't give up. Please."

He saw the tears roll down Sarah's face.

Saw her take a few breaths. Attempt to calm herself as more blood dribbled down her forehead.

"R-right," she said.

"You ready?"

"Right."

"Okay," Hayden said, turning back to the front of the car. "Okay. On my count of three. One, two ... three!"

Hayden pushed.

But he underestimated just how bad his right shoulder was hurting.

And evidently from Sarah's yelp of pain, she wasn't getting out of here anytime soon either.

The pair of them took deep breaths. Tried to recover. Tried to recover as the zombies stepped nearer, as they surrounded the car, which was filling with fumes—fumes that were triggering Hayden's long-forgotten asthma.

"We need to try again," Hayden said.

"I can't—"

"You can," Hayden said. "You can."

He didn't say anything else.

Just put his hands on the dashboard pushed right against his diaphragm.

Rested his teeth around his lips.

"On my count of three again," he said. "One, two, three!"

This time, Hayden pressed with everything he had.

Pressed through the pain.

Dug his teeth into his lips and tasted even more blood.

He heard Sarah shout beside him. Heard her shout, but still he pushed, still she pushed.

He could feel the dashboard lifting.

Now just had to get his hand to the door.

Just had to push it open.

Just had to—

He felt something grab his left hand.

Felt something drag him away.

Sharpness sinking in.

The sharpness of a zombie's fingernails.

Just their fingernails.

Please just their fingernails.

Whatever it was dragged him away from the dashboard, pulled him out through the door, cutting his chest and his belly on loose rusty metal.

And then he was outside.

Outside in the cold, clouds staring down at him.

Tons of zombies gathering around his blood-smeared body like sharks around bait.

"Fuck," Hayden muttered, trying to roll onto his side to grab something—grab anything. No sign of his wrench. And the zombies were getting closer. One of them pushing him down onto the concrete. Scratching at his body. Getting ready to sink its teeth into …

His flailing hand landed on a loose chunk of sharp glass that'd smashed away in the accident.

He swung it around just as the zombie put its mouth around his arm.

Sliced through its temple, pushed it away. Didn't sever its spinal cord but it would do. He just had to put them on the ground. All he could do right now.

He clambered to his feet in the middle of the rotting mass and swung the glass into as many zombies as he could. Felt anger with every one he hit—with every eye he burst, every throat he pierced, every temple he stabbed.

Because they were stopping him helping his friend.

Stopping him helping his *friends*.

And that was all that mattered in this world anymore. Friends.

He stabbed an old, balding creature right in its gut, ran around the side of the Civic and forced open the passenger door. The infected swarmed to the left of the car, too dumb to figure out that the right was just as legitimate a turning point.

Which was good.

It worked for Hayden.

"Sarah," he said, crouching down by the car, grabbing the top of the door.

She looked up at him. Looked up with tears in her eyes. With more blood running down her head. With resignation in her face. "You—you go," she said.

Hayden shook his head. Shook his head and stepped away from the door. Stabbed the zombie staggering towards him right in its neck, pushed it back against the rest of the crowd, toppling them over like dominos.

He crouched back by the car. "I'm not going anywhere without—"

"You have to," Sarah said. "I'm—I'm stuck. I'm stuck and you have to ... you have to get to Holly. You have to survive."

Hayden swallowed a sickly tasting lump as he stared into Sarah's eyes. Realisation welled up inside. The same realisation as when he'd left Gary behind back in the woods. The realisation that his own life was at stake here. That his very existence was on the verge of being compromised.

That everything he'd fought so hard to preserve was at risk of ending.

But if that was the case, so be it.

He stood.

"I made you a promise," he said.

Swung the glass at the next of the zombies.

And then the next.

And the next.

"I promised I wouldn't leave you."

Stabbed another zombie as more of them poured around the side of the Civic, as some of them dragged their bodies across the broken metal at the front of the car, piercing their limbs and stretching their skin in the process.

"So I'm not going anywhere," Hayden said.

He ran into the zombie standing directly opposite him.

Slammed into its rotting body and knocked it right back into its companions.

And when it fell to the floor, when it took its friends down with it, Hayden ran back to the car.

Grabbed the top of the door.

Stuck his teeth into his tongue as more zombies approached.

"I'm not going anywhere," he said.

Dragged as hard as he could.

Rusty metal scraping against the potholed concrete.

"I'm not—"

He fell back.

Didn't understand why at first. Not completely.

But then he lifted his aching head and saw the car door was open.

Sarah was just inside.

"Quick!" Hayden said.

He rushed over to Sarah. Rushed over as more zombies stepped around the car, just a metre or so away.

He grabbed her arms.

"Sorry. This ... this might hurt."

And then he dragged her out of the car as hard as he could.

Although she screamed, although she punched at his skinny ribs, he got Sarah out of the car.

He got her out of the car and wrapped an arm around her back, helped her to her feet.

And then, together, they ran as quickly as they could away from the mass of baffled zombies, towards the coach, towards Holly, towards ...

He stopped when he saw the long-haired man standing by the coach door pointing a pistol right at them.

"Well, hello there," he said. "You two look like you could do with a ride."

THIRTY-NINE

"Pop your hands behind your head and walk over this way, you two. Quick."

Hayden didn't put his hands behind his head. He just kept them by his side. Kept on gripping on to the sharp piece of glass.

Staring at the gun pointed right at him.

The footsteps of the zombies traipsing ever closer to him from behind.

He didn't want to move. Didn't want to walk into the coach—not on this lunatic's terms.

But he knew staying out here was suicide. For him. For Sarah.

Maybe the coach was suicide too, but it was somewhere.

"Come on," the straggly-haired man said, yellow-toothed grin across his face. "Hardly got time on yer side, like."

He sniggered like it was some kind of joke.

Hayden just kept on holding the glass.

Kept on staring back at this man.

"You knackered my coach. Only fair that you take a look at it with me. Help me out with the ... the repairs."

A smile stretched even wider across his face.

Behind them, as Hayden and Sarah stood there, battered and bruised from the accident, more zombies approached. They couldn't stay out here. Couldn't stay on the road.

They had to take their chances.

They had to get onto the coach.

The man lifted the gun.

Aimed it right at Sarah's head.

"Won't ask you again. Man can only be kind so many times, y'know? You wanna put yer hands behind yer heads and walk this way before I—"

"Okay," Hayden said, raising both his hands, putting them behind his head. The glass still in his palm. "Okay. We're coming."

He caught a glance of Sarah as he started walking. Saw the uncertainty in her eyes.

But she just had to walk with him.

She just had to trust him.

Sure, he didn't trust himself, but at least he was willing to try.

She walked. She walked with Hayden and then both of them were walking. Both with their hands raised. Both walking away from the zombies, who followed, getting closer and closer. Soon they'd surround the coach. Soon, there'd be no way out.

They'd die here. Hayden, Sarah, Holly, this whack-job; everyone on that coach would die.

And Hayden was leading them right towards it.

"Right," the man said when Hayden and Sarah reached the side of the coach, the zombies still following. "Now you walk up in this strict order, you hear me? The woman goes first. The sunflower, yeah. She comes up first. And—and then you. You come up. You meet my Pamela, both of yer. She's proper welcoming. Proper friendly to strangers, you know?"

Hayden looked into the eyes of the man and all he saw was madness. Insanity. Grip on reality, lost.

But he nodded because the cries of the zombies grew louder.

Because their footsteps got closer and closer …

Sarah tried to lift a hand to climb onto the ladders but she couldn't. In too much pain. Still hurting from the car accident, something broken no doubt.

"She's hurt," Hayden said.

The man just stared on, not a glimmer of pity in his eyes. Kept the pistol pointed down at Sarah, at Hayden. "Is this gonna be a problem?"

"I can come up there," Hayden said. "And then I can lift her when I'm—"

"You don' have to lift her, sir," he said, leaning out of the door and down the ladder. "I can lift pretty decent myself. Besides, Pamela's waitin'. Never wanna keep her waitin' too long. Ain't that right, honey?"

Sarah didn't say a word in response.

She just looked back at Hayden. Looked back at him and shook her head as the echoing cries of the zombies got louder, as they got within metres of the pair of them.

"Take his hand," Hayden said.

Sarah shook her head. "I can't—"

"Just take his hand," Hayden said.

He put a hand on Sarah's arm.

Slipped the sharp piece of glass into her hand.

And then he smiled at her.

She waited a second. Waited before doing anything.

And then she reached up and grabbed the man's dirty hand. His nails long and filled with soil, uncut in years, turning green.

He pulled her up and he smiled all the way.

Smiled, as Hayden put a foot on the bottom step of the ladder.

Smiled, as Hayden started climbing; climbing away from the zombies below, away from certain death.

No. Not away from certain death. Just postponing it.

There was no running from death. Never was.

Especially not in this world.

He kept on smiling right until he threw Sarah in the coach.

And then his face went serious.

He pointed the gun right at Hayden's head.

"Sorry, pal," he said, his voice barely audible over the drowning cries of the infected. "Think we're outta seats."

He smiled again.

And then he pulled the trigger.

FORTY

Hayden swore he felt the blast as the bullet pierced his face.

Swore he felt his skull explode.

But he was still thinking.

Holding onto the ladder by the tips of his fingers but still thinking.

So conscious.

So alive.

He opened his eyes. Saw the lunatic hanging down from the coach door above him, gun pointing just to the right of his head. Only he wasn't smiling, not anymore.

He wasn't smiling because a piece of glass was wedged into his left shoulder.

He wobbled forward and Hayden took his opportunity.

Reached up for the man.

Grabbed his arm and dragged him down the ladder. Tried to throw him onto the road. To hurtle him into the mouths of the hungry zombies all gathered below.

And for a moment, as the man fell past Hayden, as he went flying down the ladders and over Hayden's back, he thought he'd done it. He really thought he'd succeeded. That he'd dealt with the threat already.

But then he felt the man's hand wrap around his right ankle and drag him closer to the road.

He turned. Looked over his shoulder, gripping tight as he could onto the coach ladders. He was way too weak to support the man's weight. If he held on any longer, he'd snap Hayden's leg away. Tear it from his body.

The step Hayden held onto couldn't take the two of them. Hayden heard it creaking. Felt it slowly morphing as it dug into his fingers, as his body begged and begged him to let go.

No. He couldn't let go. Not now.

"You fucker," the man screamed, yanking harder at Hayden's leg as he dangled right above the hungry mass of zombies. "Nobody lays a fuckin' finger on my Pamela! You filthy sonna bitch lay a finger on my Pamela and there'll be—"

Hayden booted the man right in his face.

Felt flimsy yellow teeth crack on contact.

Saw blood dribble down the man's chin.

He looked up at Hayden. Looked up with anger on his typically happy face, zombies scraping at his boots, getting so closer to pulling them both even more. "Shouldn'ta done that," he said. "Shouldn'ta fucking ..."

He went quiet then, and Hayden wasn't sure why. Not at first.

And then he felt a sharp pain around his Achilles and he understood.

The man bit down on his leg. Bit down so hard that Hayden felt himself going cold, felt his muscles going numb. So this is what it feels like. This is what it feels like to be bitten. This is what it feels like to know your life is ending.

This is the sound of the time bomb ticking.

Hayden kicked back at the man. Kicked hard at his solid head, at his eyes. He kicked, and although he was in agony, although the man kept on biting on his leg, blood spraying down and sending the zombies into more of a frenzy, he kept his composure. Kept his focus.

He had to get into the coach.

He had to get to Sarah, to Holly.

And he had to get away from here.

"Hayden!"

No sooner had he thought of Sarah than he heard her voice. He looked back up the side of the coach. Saw her holding her hand down for him. Didn't look the securest of grips but Hayden would take anything right now. Anything but being stuck on here, this man's teeth wedged inside his leg, the zombies getting more and more irate.

The ladders creaking.

"Grab my hand!" Sarah shouted.

And Hayden wanted to. He wanted so much to.

But he knew grabbing Sarah's hand was too much of a risk. He'd just end up dragging her back down here. Pulling her into the jaws of the scrap; the jaws of the zombies.

No.

He had to hold on.

He had to do this himself.

He had to conquer this battle alone.

He looked back down at the man, face completely red in Hayden's blood.

He tried not to puke. Tried to keep his balance. His composure.

Took a deep breath of the putrid air.

And then he did the only thing he could.

Stepped down the ladder.

Down towards the man.

At first, as he looked down into the dizzying mass of starving zombies, Hayden was convinced he was going to fall. That there was no chance he was going to hold on. That the pain in his ankle was going to overcome him and he was going to fall to an agonising end.

But no.

He couldn't allow that to happen.

Because he had friends to look out for.

He had people to save.

So he reached down, one hand still gripped on the ladder, so tight it'd gone white.

He grabbed the filthy man's greasy, rope-like hair.

And he pulled his head back.

Hard.

Initially, Hayden stopped. He stopped because the man kept on biting down on his leg. As he moved, some of Hayden's skin split away. Blood spurted out of his torn flesh.

But fuck.

He had to keep on going.

He wanted to survive this so he had to do whatever it took.

Even if it took more agony.

He reached a little further down, the ladders creaking under his grip.

Reached to the man's eyes, which were clenched shut.

And he scratched at them.

Scratched and prodded and jabbed at them hard, as hard as he could.

And then he kicked.

Kicked and jabbed and pushed his head away even though the skin split away from his leg, even though muscle tore away, bathed the zombies below.

He kept on kicking and thought about Sarah. Thought about Holly. Kept on pushing and thought about the people he'd sworn to stand by. Sworn to protect.

He kept on kicking at the man's head.

Hoping it'd just crack like an eggshell.

Scratching at his hands as they gripped onto Hayden, desperate to knock him down to the infected below.

And for a moment, Hayden thought he had it.

As the man's grip loosened, he thought he had it.

But then he heard something crack.

Something creak.

Felt movement.

He looked back at the coach and he realised exactly what it was.

The ladder was splitting away from the coach.

He was falling into the mass of zombies below.

And there was nothing he could do about it.

FORTY-ONE

When the ladder split away from the side of the coach and creaked over the mass of zombies below, Hayden didn't feel afraid.

Not for himself. Because he was beyond worrying about himself. He'd way transgressed mere self-obsession. No. There was no worry for himself anymore, even though the sounds of the zombies scratching and gasping around below him grew louder, even as their deathly stench thickened.

He worried for Sarah. He worried for Holly.

Because he owed it to them to stay alive.

He felt the man's teeth tightening on his ankle, his grip solidifying around his lower leg, as the ladder's descent rapidly increased. He knew the coach driver would be first to go. And he was okay with that. He was completely fine with it.

Because yes, everyone deserved a chance in this world. A second chance, a third in some cases.

But this man had kidnapped Holly.

He'd tried to kill Hayden, and he'd no doubt kill Sarah—or worse—if he got the chance.

So fuck him. He deserved to die. Painfully.

He felt the man's teeth slide out of his leg, felt the mass of zombies surrounding him. "You ain't goin' nowhere without me," he shouted, blood dribbling down his chin. "I ain't leavin' my Pamela with you. Ain't no chance I'm leavin' my Pamela with you."

The bottom of the ladder clanged against the concrete.

The zombies swarmed around the pair of them like bees—angry, protective bees.

"Don't think you have a choice," Hayden said, looking the man in his eyes.

Then he pulled his foot back.

Booted him right in his face, cracking his nose.

And then he looked up at the side of the coach and he ran.

He felt the hands and the nails of the zombies scratching at him as he hurtled towards the coach door. Heard nothing but their hungry cries, and hearing them together in unison like this was almost peaceful. A drone. Like sirens readying their prey, luring them in before the inevitable, unavoidable slaughter.

And as he ran, as he hurtled towards the coach, as he kept the half-open door in his sights, Hayden thought he felt things. Sensations. Feelings on his skin he didn't understand; feelings he couldn't comprehend.

But still he ran on.

Because he had to.

That was his duty.

That was his purpose.

That was his life.

He threw himself at the bottom of the door. And despite the pain and the exhaustion crippling his body, he pulled himself up. Pulled himself up with his weak arms that used to always win him the nickname "Noodle Arms" back in high school P.E. classes. Arms he'd strived over and over again to bulk up, to make more attractive to those around him, to himself, but always lost the motivation whenever a spliff and a few cans of beer crept along.

Now, they lifted him.

Now, Noodle Arms dragged him up to the door.

Now—

He felt and heard two things.

First thing was the dragging at his leg. The opposite leg to the one that the psycho nut job had bitten. Something pulling him back down to the road below.

Second thing—the thing he heard—was the psycho's scream.

As he gripped the side of the coach, he looked back. Saw the psycho in the middle of the zombies. Saw them sinking their teeth into his head. Thumbing around his eyes, sticking their bony fingers inside his mouth and splitting it apart.

Butchering him.

And the look of fear in his eyes.

The common look that everyone had in their eyes when certain death approached, good or evil, right or wrong.

Terror.

And then his eyes were gone.

Burst.

Bitten.

And Hayden was left to deal with the lone zombie clinging to his ankle, stretching his muscles on the verge of splitting.

He looked down at the zombie. Looked down at it with its greying face, its loose skin.

He kicked at it. Kicked at it and noticed its flesh dropping away like dead rotting fish upon contact. Saw bone underneath as the muscle split away, the signs of wear and ageing there to see.

He kicked even though blood dripped out of his leg, even though more zombies gathered around him, even though he went dizzy with blood loss or pain or both or neither, he wasn't sure, he couldn't be sure.

He kicked even though the zombie's grip got tighter.

Kicked and held on to the side of the coach even though his fingers got sweatier.

He kicked until the zombie let go.

Just for a millisecond, it let go.

And then he tensed with every muscle in his body.

Dragged himself up through the side door of the coach, inside the vehicle.

Before he looked inside, he took a glance back in the psycho driver's direction. Couldn't see him anymore. Couldn't hear him begging. And Hayden figured it was horrible that ultimately, that's how it ended for everyone. That was the sharp end that everyone faced eventually. Screaming then silenced. Everything then nothing.

Alive, then dead.

Like a light bulb bursting. Unexpected but inevitable.

He turned back to the coach.

Looked into the darkness.

Swallowed a lump in his throat.

Now, he had to get to Holly.

Now, he had to make sure Sarah was okay.

Now, he had to …

His thoughts trailed off when he heard a cry to his right.

FORTY-TWO

The first thing Hayden noticed as he stepped inside the coach was the smell.

It wasn't like the normal stench of rot he'd grown so used to living in this world of decay. No, it was sicklier. A sourness that clung to his nostrils—that made his head spin—made him want to puke. And although he couldn't be completely sure of what'd gone on in here, it didn't take a whole load of imagination to work out that the psycho driver had probably done some pretty rotten things.

The taste of sweat in the air.

The sour stench of death.

And the cry.

The muffled cry right from the back of the coach, right in the darkness.

A woman's cry.

Hayden's heart picked up. He swallowed heavily. As he climbed up the sticky steps and to the middle of the coach, he wasn't sure he wanted to look down the aisle. Wasn't sure he wanted to see the source of the cry.

Holly.

Or Sarah.

Or maybe neither of those two. Maybe this "Pamela" the driver spoke of. Maybe ...

He heard the cry again.

And this time he knew he couldn't avoid turning.

He knew he just had to look.

When he looked down the aisle, Hayden wasn't exactly sure what he was seeing. How could he be? How could anyone be when faced with such violence, such brutality? Such incomprehensible acts of cruelty.

But he looked and he forced himself to keep on looking.

He had a duty to keep on looking.

Down the aisle, in each and every one of the seats, women. Some of them fully grown. Some of them barely out of their teens.

All of them strapped into the coach.

All of them with their legs open as wide as their eyes.

Their pained, fearful eyes.

All of them with lacerations, bruises, bite marks.

Intestines dangling out of some of their torsos.

Necks slit of others.

Flies circling all of them, oblivious to the horrors around, just getting on with their airborne lives like nothing had changed.

Hayden felt his chest welling up as he limped down the aisle of the coach. He didn't want to look at the passengers but he had to. He had to because he couldn't keep on pulling the wool over his eyes, not any longer. No matter how much he insisted desensitisation was a bad thing—something he'd never come back from—he had to look because he had to understand the kind of cruelty out there in the world.

Because sure, Holly had double-crossed him. She'd tried to kill Sarah.

But she'd done it because she was trying to get back to her husband.

She'd done it because she was afraid.

Not like this. This was just pure cruelty. This was evil.

This was the world they lived in now, and the world they had to stand against.

He stepped over squishy pieces of flesh. Flies head butted him. Outside, Hayden heard the familiar sound of tearing. Of damp body parts stretching and flesh splitting away. A sound as common and familiar as birdsong used to be.

Hayden couldn't remember the last time he'd heard birdsong. Not long ago, he used to hear it. Peaceful, reassuring, calming.

He couldn't remember the last time he'd noticed true beauty.

As he made his way down the aisle, closer and closer to the back, anxious about what he might find, Hayden noticed something. Something lying on the floor in the middle. A body. A woman's body.

No.

A girl's body.

She was blonde. Lying there all rigid and cold in the middle of the floor. Blood drooling out of a crack in her skull. A crack that looked recent. A crack that—

"Hayden."

The voice startled him. Jolted him out of his trance. He lifted his head. Looked down the aisle. Looked right to the back of the vehicle.

He saw Sarah kneeling right by a seat at the back of the coach.

Holding someone's hand.

Someone's limp, still hand.

He forced a smile at Sarah and took a few painful steps closer to her, blood still seeping out of his ankle. He felt his heart pounding. Prepared for the condition he might find Holly in. Because her hand looked still. Her arm looked pale. And as he climbed over the fallen girl, he started to put together a sequence of events in his mind.

The girl had chased Holly to the back of the coach.

Sarah had stopped her.

But she'd been too late.

She'd been too ...

When he saw Holly sitting upright in the back seat of the coach, tears rolling down her face but life in her eyes, Hayden stopped.

She looked at him in a way he couldn't quite get his head around. Not like she was dying. Not like she knew she was dying. But like she was sad. Sad about something.

Sad about someone.

Sad about ...

It was then that he saw it.

That he saw the bite marks.

Saw them on her arm.

"You—you two should get away from here," Sarah said.

Hayden felt his throat tighten up. Felt tears welling up in his eyes. "Sarah, you—"

"We did it, Hayden," she said, a smile on her face, but tears rolling down her cheeks. "We got to her. We saved her. Now you have to get out of here."

She said it with such certainty as she held onto Holly's hand.

Such authority and fearlessness.

But that didn't change the fact.

It didn't change the truth as Hayden stood there, flies buzzing around him, pain splitting through his leg, zombies groaning outside as they pursued their next prey.

It didn't change the bite mark.

The bite mark on Sarah's left forearm.

FORTY-THREE

"Please, Hayden. The two of you. You ... you have to leave. It's just how it is now."

Sarah's words dulled in Hayden's mind. They were distorted, like how he imagined voices to be while underwater. Not that he'd know. He'd always been afraid of submerging himself underwater.

Right now, staring at the bite mark on Sarah's left forearm, he felt like he was drowning.

"We made it this far so we—"

"We can sort it," Hayden said, stepping towards Sarah, then taking a step back, unsure of where to look, where to go, what to do.

Sarah just kept on smiling. Eyes glistening. "We can't," she said. "Not—not this. We can't sort this—"

"Your arm," Hayden said, heart racing as he searched the seats of the coach, rooted through the decaying bodies, the smell doing nothing to affect him, not anymore. "We—we can cut it. We can cut it off above the bite wound and—"

"No," Sarah said.

Hayden turned back. Looked her in her beautiful eyes.

"No you can't," she said.

He understood right then. Felt the news blow into his core. Crash against him. She wasn't telling him it was physically impossible that chopping her arm off might stave away the infection. She was telling him that he didn't have her permission. That she wasn't allowing it.

She wasn't going to let him help her.

"But I ... I don't want to give up on you," Hayden said.

The words hurt. And Hayden saw the words hurt Sarah too. Saw more tears drip down her face. Holly sat beside her, crying too. Holding Sarah's hand. Shaking her head.

"You have to now," Sarah said. "You just have to."

"Maybe we can—"

"Hayden," Sarah said, raising her hand. "It's over."

He put a hand through his greasy hair. Heart racing. Throat swelling up. Sarah. The first person he'd known in this new world. The last remaining friend he had. The woman who'd saved him back on the first day.

The woman he'd travelled so far with. Who he'd lost so much with. Who'd stood beside him and held his hand as together they conquered the world.

Who put her arms around him when he needed to talk.

About his mum. About his dad.

About his sister.

Bitten.

Anger replaced the sadness. Anger towards Holly. Because it was her fault they were in here in the first place. Her fault for betraying them. Her fault they'd left Riversford and ended up in this fucking hell. "It shouldn't be you," Hayden said to Sarah while looking at Holly. "It—it just shouldn't be—"

"But it is," Sarah said. She stared down at the blood dripping from her arm, her face growing a little paler, fear filling it for the briefest of moments.

And then she looked up at Hayden and she smiled shakily again. "It just is."

Hayden felt sick. Wasn't sure if it was the smell or the pain in his leg or Sarah or Holly or just fucking everything. But he felt sick. So sick he needed to puke. So disoriented. So lost. "What do ... What're we supposed to do?"

Sarah glanced at Holly then back at Hayden. "You—you do what you came here to do."

"But Holyhead's—"

"You take Holly back there. To—to her guy. You do what you came to do. The right thing."

Hayden thought about Holyhead. Thought about that bastion of hope that was now nothing more than a black cloud of uncertainty. "And ... and what then?"

Sarah didn't say anything to that.

She didn't say anything and Hayden knew exactly why.

She didn't know.

Holly would find her ex and Hayden would be alone a hundred miles from "home."

Holly wouldn't find her ex and Hayden would still be alone.

Lost.

"You're strong, Hayden. Weak as shit when we first met but a hell of a lot stronger since."

Hayden shook his head as he stepped closer to Sarah. As he crouched opposite her. "I'm not."

"You are," she said, grabbing his hand, squeezing it. Holly continued to cry beside Sarah. Tears of guilt. "You're the strongest, most dedicated and loyal man I've ever met. And ... well, sure, I've not met many loyal men in my life. But you're one of the good ones. Don't you ever forget that."

Hayden wanted to say something back to Sarah.

Then he felt her lips on his.

Tasted her sweat.

The bitterness of her tears.

But savoured every ounce of warmth that filled up inside.

After the kiss that felt like it lasted forever, Sarah backed away. She wiped her eyes. Turned to Holly, who refused to look at her.

"I can't ever forget. What—what you did to me. What you tried to do to me. But I believe deep down you're a good person. Good, but just scared like everyone else."

She grabbed Holly's face.

Turned her neck so she was looking right at her.

"Don't you dare betray Hayden again or I swear I'll come back and fucking bite you myself."

Holly didn't say a word.

She just kept on sniffing.

Kept on crying.

Her visible guilt said more than any words ever could.

The fingernails of the zombies scratched at the sides of the coach. Made the vehicle rock from side to side. Hayden wasn't sure how long all three of the group sat there—the group that was dwindling, fracturing, fragmenting—but he wished it'd just last forever. Like a pause button on life. He wanted to live in those flickering paused moments of old VCRs.

But this was no home video. This was life. And like everything in life, Hayden had to make a decision. He couldn't crawl back into the stasis of his pre-apocalyptic existence.

"How do you want to go?" he asked. Wasn't sure how he managed to ask the question. It ripped him to shreds inside. Broke him down.

But he had to be brave.

He had to be strong.

He had to do what was right.

Because if Sarah wanted something—if anyone close wanted something—he had to deliver it.

Sarah puffed her lips out. Smiled. "Hardly got the best options, eh? But I dunno. I think the nutter who drove this thing might have a spare gun lying around somewhere. That'd be my preference. Failing that, a ..." She stopped. Gulped. "A blade to the neck would—would finish me of course."

A flashback to Clarice.

To the way she'd died. The way she'd been murdered.

"I'm not doing that," Hayden said. "I ... I can't do that. Nobody deserves that."

"Don't always get what we deserve, boyo," Sarah said. "Surely you've realised that by now."

Hayden stood up. Walked down the aisle. He looked from side to side for a gun or for something that'd make it ... that'd make *death* easier for Sarah. Because she'd made her choice. She'd made her choice and he had to honour that.

But he didn't find a gun.

All he found was broken glass. Pieces of scrap metal. A blood-soaked knife.

He looked at the knife as it rested on the lap of a disembowelled brunette. Looked at it and imagined wrapping his hands around it. Imagined lifting it, walking back to Sarah, crouching opposite her, holding her hand and looking her in the eye as he pressed it to her throat—or her chest, maybe her chest would be better, right in the heart, but he didn't know where the heart was exactly so he—

Shit. He couldn't fucking do this. He wasn't fucking doing this.

He stepped away from the chair and he walked down the aisle, away from Sarah, away from Holly.

"Where you going?" Sarah asked.

Hayden kept on walking. Towards the open door. Towards the breeze.

And a part of him wanted to jump back outside. Back out of his responsibilities. Away from his duty, just like he'd been doing all his life.

But instead, he sat down in the damp driver's seat. Felt the piss of the fallen driver soaking through his trousers.

He turned the key and he started up the engine.

"Hayden, what're you—"

"I'm not leaving you behind. I respect your right to die but … but not like this."

He put the coach into gear. Started reversing.

"But you—you can't even fucking drive," Sarah said.

"You're right," he said, as he swerved the coach away from the zombies, knocking a few of them over in the process. "But I suppose I'm just gonna have to learn. 'Cause I'm not leaving you behind."

He continued his three—or zillion—point turn. Continued until the road to Holyhead was back ahead of him. Until the sun shone through the dusty, bloody window, marking the road ahead.

"We're going to Holyhead. Whatever's there, we're finishing this journey. And we're finishing it together."

FORTY-FOUR

"This—this is it. This is where he lives."

Hayden pushed a foot on the brake of the monstrous coach. For a first shot at driving since failing his lessons miserably in his late teens—mostly through lack of motivation, surprise surprise—he hadn't done so bad.

He'd got Holly to Holyhead. He'd got Sarah there, too.

They'd made it. Together.

But how much further they went together was the new question.

"Want me to take a look inside?" Hayden asked.

Holly placed a hand on his shoulder. Shook her head. "It's okay. I should—"

"Together," Hayden said. "That's how I said we'd do it. That's —that's a promise I'm keeping."

Holly looked back at Hayden right in the eyes. Looked for a moment like she was going to protest.

Then, she sighed and she nodded.

"Right," Holly said, leading the way to the coach exit. "Together it is."

Hayden helped Sarah out of the coach. She was bitten, sure,

going colder and paler, sweating like mad. But she seemed okay. Seemed in good spirits. Seemed ... prepared, amazingly. And Hayden wondered how anyone could be prepared for a fate like hers that lay ahead. For the uncertainty within the certainty. For now they knew what followed death. Death wasn't a mystery anymore. The afterlife, that was clear. It roamed the streets and tore people to pieces.

No. The uncertainty now was whether you wanted an afterlife or not.

That was the greatest choice of all.

"You okay?" Hayden asked.

Sarah winced as they hopped off the coach and into the fresh Holyhead air. "Just about. How's your leg?"

"Fine," Hayden said, even though he was biting his tongue just to keep the pain from his injured Achilles at bay. There were bigger matters at stake right now. Bigger things to worry about. "Just hope she finds what she's looking for."

Sarah wiped the dust from her torn jeans. "You know too well that sometimes it's best not to find what you're looking for. Nothing wrong with a little hope."

She had a point. Was finding his mum and dad really the right thing? And Clarice? Would it've just been better if he'd believed they were still out there, still surviving, making it?

No.

No, he didn't believe that was true.

"Hope's good. But reality's more important."

He took Sarah's hand and together they walked down the pavement in pursuit of Holly.

The suburban area of Holyhead they were in was pretty much like every other suburb Hayden had seen since the fall. Empty. Quiet. No sign of life behind the windows of detached houses. Coke cans scraping across the concrete in the breeze. Empty bottles lying half-cracked, lined with blood, a sign of a recent fight. Weeds sprouting up from the middle of the uncut gardens

—gardens that would never be touched again. The smell of decay from overturned rubbish bins, left on the pavement but never to be collected.

Holly was right in front of a detached house just a few metres away. And as Hayden approached, Sarah's hand in his, he remembered Newbie. The hope in Newbie's eyes when he'd gone upstairs; found evidence that his family were alive.

But then the fate that had befallen him.

All because he wasn't looking over his shoulder.

All because he was blissfully oblivious to his surroundings.

Holly started walking up the cobbled pathway. "I'll go check—"

"Not alone," Hayden said, limping up beside her. "Not come all this way to risk losing you on the doorstep."

Holly frowned when she looked at Hayden.

Then she shook her head.

"What?" Hayden asked.

"Nothing."

"That look. What was it?"

Holly looked back at Hayden. Then at Sarah. She took a deep breath then cleared her throat. "The pair of you. You ... you don't have to be this nice. I don't deserve you to be this—this understanding. Not for how I treated you. For what I did to you."

Hayden nodded. Forced a smile. "Maybe not. But it's all we've got right now. So we're here with you."

He held a hand out. A hand pointed in the direction of Holly's ex's house.

Holly smiled back at him.

Walked up the pathway.

Towards the front door.

Hayden and Sarah followed.

Listened to their footsteps echo in the silence.

Holly stopped right in front of the door. Lifted her fist to knock, then lowered it. Put it on the handle. Started to turn. "He always said I was welcome to visit. That—that we'd always be friends no matter what happened. Guess we'll find out if he really meant it."

The handle reached the bottom.

Holly pushed the door open.

The first thing that hit Hayden, as usual, was the smell.

The smell of rotting that always brought negative connotations along with it.

Because rotting meant death.

And death meant failure.

But despite the smell, despite the similarly familiar sound of insects buzzing around, Hayden and Sarah followed Holly inside.

Followed her to the closed lounge door.

Followed her every step.

Hayden's heart picked up when Holly pushed open the lounge door. Nothing in there. Nothing but a big television, of photos of a man and a woman, presumably Andy and his new wife, all standing on a fireplace. No sign of life. No sign of death. Nothing.

So it came to the stairs.

It always came to the stairs.

The creaking of the steps as they walked up, one by one.

Just like they'd creaked when Hayden found his big sister Annabelle hanging all those years ago.

Just like they'd creaked when he'd walked up the stairs to find his mum and dad, Dad turned, Mum on her way, in that little box room at the front of Clarice's house.

Just like they creaked in his nightmares.

Step by step by step.

They reached the top step. Still no sign of blood, of anything like that. But still no sign of life. The torture of finding a loved one dead versus the torture of not knowing whether they'd made it or not.

But that wouldn't be the case. Not today.

Because the smell of decay was growing stronger the closer they got to the white door opposite the stairs.

Holly stopped before it. Teeth rattling together. Shaking all over.

Hayden put a hand on her shoulder. She flinched a little, then let it rest there, let it rest there as she stared at the door, prepared to look at the inevitable, to face her demons head on.

"It'll be okay," Hayden said. "Whatever happens, it'll be okay."

She swallowed a lump in her throat.

Nodded.

Lifted her hand.

Put it on the door handle.

Hayden's heart picking up now too.

Smell of decay intensifying, sound of flies—

"H-Holly?"

The voice came from the left. A man's voice. Made Hayden flinch and reach into his pocket instinctively, such was the nature of the world now.

Hayden turned. So too did Sarah, Holly.

A man stood staring at them. He had a long, rusty knife in his hand. His skin was pink and bruised, his hair long and unkempt, his dark beard unshaven, interspersed with bits of ginger, bits of white.

He looked at Holly with tired, bloodshot eyes.

And in those eyes, Hayden saw the man he'd seen in the pictures downstairs. The man he'd seen in the photographs. A fragment of him still remaining in this malnourished man in a loose white (or off-grey) cotton shirt, black trousers, no shoes.

"Andy?" Holly said. "Andy?"

She didn't say anything else.

Neither did he.

They both walked towards each other.

Hurtled into each other's arms.

And together, they embraced one another tightly and they cried.

Because they'd found one another.

Holly's mission was complete.

Hayden and Sarah's mission was complete.

And although he was happy for them—although he *should've* been happy for them—Hayden really wasn't sure how to feel.

Other than afraid.

FORTY-FIVE

Hayden held Sarah's shaking hand and watched as Holly and Andy smiled, caught up, made up for lost time.

It was nice, in a way. Nice seeing two people who were completely adrift from one another put the past behind them and push forward. Sitting in this lounge and watching Holly and Andy talk, it was clear there was still a spark between them. And there was no excusing the bad things Holly had done, sure. But right now Hayden saw nothing but a woman delighted to be back in the company of someone she knew. Someone she loved.

And Andy looked just as delighted to be back with Holly.

"Not been easy surviving out here," Andy said, turning to look at Hayden and Sarah. "Impossible to know when the dead're coming and when they're taking a breather for the day. But y'know."

"Something you just get used to," Hayden said.

"Right," Andy said, nodding.

He looked right into Hayden's eyes like he was scanning him. Checking he was legit. A look everyone exchanged with one another these days. Because he cared about Holly. He wanted to know Hayden hadn't hurt her. That Sarah hadn't hurt her. He'd stitched up and bandaged Hayden's leg, but that didn't mean he trusted him. Trust was a dangerous thing, Hayden knew that as well as anyone.

Hayden didn't mention Holly's lies. Her attempts to leave them behind—to kill them.

They were the past. This was the present.

She'd made her mistakes. She'd done what she'd done. And after all, in the end, it'd got her home. Back with the man she loved.

The wrong methods, sure, but the right outcome.

Hayden shuddered to think what that said about the wider world now in general.

"You folks travelled far?" Andy asked.

"Too far," Sarah said. Her speech was slurred. Sweat dripped down her face. But she was holding on.

Holding on, but dying.

But holding on.

"But we got here," she continued, every word a pained effort. "So ... so it was worth it."

She exchanged a glance with Holly.

Holly nodded back at her.

"You guys can stay around here," Andy said, peeking out of the closed curtain, which cast a pink hue over the room. "Plenty of places for you to stay. Spare beds, shit like that. Just avoid the door at the top of the stairs. Deterrent. You probably smelled it. Ain't permanent but it does the trick. Keeps looters wary long enough for me to ... to sort 'em out."

"You've been alone all this time?" Sarah asked.

Andy nodded. "Well, since ... since my wife disappeared. Ran off with the next door neighbour. Never did trust her."

"Taste of your own medicine," Holly said.

Andy shrugged. "Maybe so. Maybe so."

Hayden stood up. Walked around the lounge. Looked at the family photographs. Snapshots of happiness. Fossils from the world before. "We know a place. Back up north. Decent place with good walls where we've been staying for a while. Holly knows it. It won't be an easy journey back but you should join us. There's good people there. There's—"

"I'm not coming back, Hayden."

Hayden turned around. Looked into Holly's eyes. And as she stared up at him he felt his worst fears coming true. Holly refusing to return to Riversford because she had what she wanted, *who* she wanted.

Sarah dying.

Leaving him alone.

Completely, utterly alone.

"I've made it this far to be with Andy."

"Riversford's safer—"

"Perhaps," Holly said. She put an arm around Andy. "But it's not *here*."

Hayden looked at her a little longer. Begged she'd change her mind. Pleaded silently for her and Andy to scrap their plans of staying put, to move back to Riversford with him, to start again.

"I've travelled too far," Holly said. "I … I've done too many things on the road. Things I'm—I'm not proud of. To get here. I can't do that again. I can't … I can't allow myself to lose it like that again. I'm sorry."

Hayden understood it. He understood Holly's reluctance to step back into a world that corrupted her in the first place. He understood her adamance to stay away from that dangerous world that almost killed her.

"If this is where it ends for me then this is where it ends," Holly said, moving her hand to Andy's, holding it. "I'm tired of running. Tired of—of trying to find 'safe places' that don't exist—"

"But Riversford's—"

"Safe. For now. Right. But for how long?"

Hayden couldn't answer.

He swallowed the lump in his throat and walked over to Holly, to Andy. He crouched opposite them. Heart racing. Wanted to just beg Holly to come with him. To beg Andy to make her change her mind.

But he realised how selfish he was being.

Because he was thinking about himself. Worrying about being alone.

"But like Andy said," Holly said. "You're welcome to stay here."

Hayden looked back at Holly. He wanted to say yes. To say he'd stay here. To give up the pursuit of somewhere safe—somewhere completely safe.

But he couldn't.

"This is your home now, but it's not mine. You understand that more than anyone, I think."

He put an arm around Holly's back.

Hugged her, then pulled away.

And then he took Andy's hand. Shook it.

"Look after each other. Promise me that."

Andy smiled. "We'll do our best. You know where we are."

"Yeah," Hayden said, still holding Andy's hand. "Yeah I do."

He stepped away. Stepped away and saw Sarah standing there. So pale. So weak. Dying. The one person he had left, the one person who'd stand beside him in pursuit of a safe haven, fading away.

Sarah stepped up to Holly. Looked her in the eyes. And as Hayden walked away, walked to the lounge door, he saw them exchange a few words. Didn't know what they said exactly, but they were words that made Sarah hug Holly. Made her hug her and hold her for ages.

And then she pulled away, tears in Holly's eyes, and she stepped away.

"Don't—don't forget where we are," Holly said.

Hayden took Sarah's hand. Walked out of the lounge. Through

to the main door. "We won't." But somehow he didn't think he'd ever be back here again. And somehow, he knew Holly understood that.

Some wounds could be forgiven but they could never be healed.

He opened the door.

Felt the cool spring breeze brush against him.

Tightened his grip on Sarah's hand.

"You ready?" he asked.

She gulped. Forced a smile. "Ready—ready as I'll ever be."

Hayden leaned over. Kissed her on the cheek.

Then he stepped out of Holly and Andy's new house, out onto the pathway, out into the unknown.

He couldn't look back.

Only ahead.

And immediately ahead was Sarah.

Granting her wishes.

Helping her die.

FORTY-SIX

Hayden held Sarah's hand as they looked out to sea and he wished circumstances could be different.

They were at the South Stack lighthouse. Nice spot by the cliffs overlooking the Irish Sea. The sun was descending, its light glimmering in the ripples. Looked almost peaceful. Almost beautiful. And although Hayden knew Ireland was across the sea, although he knew that more land was out there—land that had no doubt fallen just like Britain—he felt like he was staring off into a peaceful oblivion. A perfect nothingness where beyond the horizon, nothing bad existed, not really.

He smelled the sea air, listened to the waves crashing against the cliffs below, and he tried not to think about Sarah's shaking hand.

It was growing colder by the second. Sarah was shivering more, too. Shivering and complaining of dizziness. Letting out little pained noises—noises that when Hayden asked about them, she rebuked, pretended all was well, all was okay.

But it wasn't okay.

It wasn't okay because Sarah was bitten.

It wasn't okay because Sarah was dying.

It wasn't okay because soon, Hayden would be alone, completely alone, and Sarah would be gone.

"I guess this is it then," she said.

The words made Hayden's stomach turn. Words he didn't want to hear. Words that shattered the false illusion of normality—no, *better* than normality—that the silence provided.

The words that confirmed Sarah was still dying. That they had a job to do, both of them. That time was of the essence.

"I'm ... I'm not sure I can stand by and—"

"It's over, Hayden. You know that as well as—as I do now. You can see it. See it in my eyes and in my body. The—the way I am. In my speech. In everything. You ... you know it now."

And Hayden did know it. As he looked at Sarah, looked into her tearful eyes, he did know it. She was going. Close to gone. But she hadn't been torn apart, not like the majority of people did, the unfortunate end they faced.

She'd made it to the edge of this cliff.

Made it to the end of land.

To a dignified death.

A death of her own making.

"I just ... I just don't think I can—"

"You said we were together. All of us. You said we'd all conquer things together. You promised that to me."

"But this isn't conquering anything."

"That's where you're wrong," she said.

She moved closer to Hayden. Put her arms around his back. He felt what little warmth was in her twitching body seeping through into him and begged it to go back inside her, to keep her heated and alive a little longer.

"This is me conquering—conquering what should happen to me. The—the infection."

"You're not. This is—this is giving up. We can still try—"

"I'm conquering it because I'd rather die than come back as one of those things." There was anger in her voice now. An impatience that hadn't been present for days. "I ... I always thought I was scared shitless of death. But right now... right now anything's better than what'll happen if I leave it. If we leave it."

Hayden's heart pounded. The taste of sea air made him sickly. He knew Sarah was right. He knew arguing with her was fickle. Pointless. Selfish.

Sarah looked down the side of the cliff. Into the sea. Looked at it with cautious curiosity.

"There's no guarantee it'll work this way."

"There's no guarantee it'll work any way," Sarah said. "But this is the way I choose. I ... I always heard it was more peaceful. Most peaceful death of all. Painful as shit for a while—water filling up your lungs, all that. But then the endorphins kick in and you don't feel anything. Nothing—nothing but softness. And then everything just seems ... seems okay."

"You can't know this for sure."

"Rather this than any other way," Sarah said.

Hayden looked back out at the sea. He lifted his hand, wiped a tear from his eyes. "You ... you don't have to do this."

"You know I do."

"I don't—I don't want you to go."

Sarah grabbed Hayden's hand. Squeezed it, tight. "You're the strongest person I've ever met. You'll make it somehow. You'll find a way."

She leaned over and kissed him and Hayden kissed her back. Didn't matter that she tasted of sweat, light tang of blood to the kiss, he switched off from all that noise and imagined he was kissing Sarah in a world where everything was good, an alternate world where all was okay.

And then he pulled away and he knew it wasn't.

He knew that wasn't reality.

And he had to accept it.

He stroked her greasy hair. Saw her eyes getting more bloodshot, her pupils dilating. A horrible way to go. A way she didn't deserve. A way nobody deserved.

So really he was the selfish one for trying to stop her going some other way.

He was the selfish one for not wanting to be alone.

He was the selfish one for denying Sarah her peace.

"I remember when we first met," she said.

"Oh not this again."

"You were so scared. So fucking terrified. But you made it this far. You made it here. In—in spite of all the shit you've faced you made it here. And I made it here too. Thanks to you."

Hayden held Sarah again. Held her and didn't want to let go.

But he had to let go.

He had to let go cause she pushed him back, gently.

Held his hands with her cold, pale fingers.

Looked right into his eyes.

"I know some people might—might roll their eyes when you go on about finding safety but I believe in you. I—Even though Holyhead's not been the place, I know you'll find the place. You'll find it 'cause you don't give up. And more people will walk with you. More people'll see how fucking …"

She stopped. Her throat clogging up. Looked out to sea.

Then back at Hayden. "More people'll see how fucking *good* you are."

She let go of one of his hands. Kept holding on to his left hand. The wind getting stronger, her feet moving closer to the cliff edge.

"So you go back to Riversford. Or you keep on looking for some kind of—of safe haven. You do whatever you have to do. Just stay yourself. 'Cause yourself is fucking amazing, Hayden McCall."

She loosened her grip on his left hand.

Stepped further away from him, closer to the edge.

Hayden wanted to beg Sarah not to make the step. Not to walk over the edge and into the sea below. He heard birdsong. Heard seagulls cawing. Noticed them stronger and more prominent than he had in weeks.

A beautiful scene, as he held Sarah's hand in the gaze of the lighthouse.

As the sun glistened on the waves, the waves rippled against the cliffs.

"I wouldn't be what I am without you," Hayden said.

Sarah smiled. She laughed a little. Laughed with that pale, shaky mouth of hers. Grinned with those lips, all chapped and blue.

She opened her mouth to say something else.

And then she pulled her hand away and stepped off the edge of the cliff.

Hayden saw the light reflecting in the sea. The seagulls swooping down and singing in the glow of the late afternoon sun. He tasted sea salt. Smelled the freshness of the rain-soaked grass beneath him.

But most of all, he felt the warmth on his fingertips.

The warmth where Sarah had held on.

The warmth that he had to hold onto—that he had to treasure —forever.

To remember Sarah.

To keep her close.

He stared out at the horizon, stared into the burning eye of the slowly descending sun.

Convinced himself he wasn't alone. That he was never alone. Never would be alone.

Even when he heard the crack against the rocks.

Even when he heard the thud against the water.

Even when he looked down at the sea and saw nothing.
Nothing but ripples illuminating in the glow of the sun.
He convinced himself he wasn't alone.
Convinced himself he wasn't alone.
Convinced himself he—

FORTY-SEVEN

Martha looked out at the movement in the trees and wondered if her daughter and she would ever get a moment's peace.

She lay flat on the rooftop of the old CityFast hangar. She held the rifle's scope to her right eye—even though her right eye was dodgy and blurry, albeit a whole lot better than her left eye, which left much to be desired. She wasn't the best shot either. Bloody hell, she hadn't even *fired* a gun before the dead decided to get up off their bums and start eating people.

But she had to do what she had to do. To protect her Amy. To keep the dead away.

She looked around at the vast expanse of trees beyond the fields, trying to find the source of the movement. Usually, it was just one or two errant infected. They found their way to the gates of Riversford where Martha popped a bullet through them, gifted them with the sleep they bloody well deserved. And every time she saw movement, a sense of hope ignited inside her. A sense of hope that maybe Hayden and the others were back. That maybe they'd found their way to Holyhead—or wherever the bloody hell they were going—and they'd brought that help back here.

Because sure, what her and her daughter had here was nice. It was safe. It was *home* now.

But she missed the company of others. And as good a kid as Amy was, it'd be nice to have someone else around for her daughter. A bit of company. Someone to help get her out of her hair.

She kept on looking at the entrance to the woods. She'd definitely seen movement. Definitely seen something twitching behind the branches. But it wouldn't be the first bloody time she'd thought she'd seen something that wasn't there. Dodgy eyes, that's what it was. Dodgy eyes and loneliness. She was getting too old for this. Way too bloody old for this.

Another part of Martha hoped that maybe somehow Newbie would find his way here. Because sure, things had happened between her and him. The proverbial shit had absolutely gone down. But it all seemed so … so fickle, now. So irrelevant in the wider context of the world, of how it was.

But she knew Newbie wasn't coming.

And chances were Hayden wasn't coming back, either.

So she kept her aim focused on the entrance of the woods and waited for a sign of movement again.

She heard her stomach churn and imagined the spices of one of those old stews Newbie used to make. Fiery chicken, delicious vegetables and sauces. Nothing against the stacks of canned soup here—they were better than nothing—but her taste buds longed for a delicious gourmet treat.

Or, well. Just something other than soup would be good.

Martha was so deep in the fantasy of succulent, delicious food that she almost missed the figure stumbling out through the trees.

She snapped out of her fantasy, overrode her tastebuds with nothing but pure, present-rooted concentration. She aimed at the figure. A man. In a black suit. With … with a cross around his neck. Dark hair. Very little blood on his clothing. Very clean cut for that matter.

And …

Martha swallowed a lump in her throat.

The man was looking right up at the lens.

Right at her.

He must've realised Martha saw him because he raised his hands. No guns in either hand. No blood on them. No weapons. Nothing but a gold ring glinting in the sunlight.

"You don't have to shoot," the man called, and the reality of his existence dawned on Martha; the understanding built inside her: this was a live man. Not an infected. A live man.

But something about that unsettled her.

And that was Amy, down in the centre of the CityFord car park, playing hopscotch.

Martha pointed the rifle back at the man. Steadied her aim. "Keep walking. Don't think I won't shoot—"

"I don't think there'll be any need for that."

The voice didn't come from the man.

No. It came from behind her.

Right behind her.

She lowered her aim.

Swung around.

Another man, this one with dark skin, with a balding head. But those same clothes. A suit. A cross around his neck. Gold ring on his finger.

Martha lifted the gun. "Who the hell are you and how the hell did you get inside?"

The man just looked into Martha's eyes.

Smiled.

Such a calming, confident, self-assured smile, even though a gun rested on his chest.

And then, "I'm Daniel. It's a pleasure to meet you."

He held out a hand.

Martha didn't budge.

He shook his head. Took his hand back. Smile stayed on his face. "You won't need your gun. We aren't going to hurt you."

"That's usually what someone says when—"

"—They're about to hurt you. Right. But we're different."

It was at that moment that Martha saw movement in the corners of her eyes. More of these men in suits, some women too, of all ages, all genders. Disorienting, like some kind of weird dream; a dream she wasn't even sure she wanted to wake up from because she was too interested in the conclusion.

"Do you have a name?" Daniel asked.

"I won't ask you again. What the hell are you—"

"And I won't tell you again," Daniel said, smile widening. "We have no intention of hurting you, so you really don't need that gun."

Martha held the gun to Daniel's chest a little longer.

And then something made her lower it.

Foolish, probably, but she wanted to hear this guy out. She wanted to understand what he was saying. Why he and his people were inside Riversford. How they'd got in here. What they wanted.

Daniel put his hands behind his back. Smiled. "Thank you. I appreciate that. Now I need you to understand that what I'm about to tell you might change things. It might alarm you, somewhat. But I'd urge you to keep your calm. I'd beg you not to panic."

Martha's heartbeat raced. She lifted her gun again. Looked around at the people surrounding her. The people in black. The people with the crosses. "Who—who are you?"

Daniel raised his hands again. That reassuring smile returned to his face. "It would help if we knew your name."

"Why does my name matter?"

"It doesn't. But I've told you my name, so I feel it's only fair."

Hesitation. No response from Martha. The sound of her heartbeat echoing in her skull.

Then, "Martha."

"Martha," Daniel said, nodding. "It's a pleasure to meet you,

Martha. I have something to show you. Something I believe you'll be very interested in seeing."

He stepped aside and before Martha could even comprehend what was happening, she saw the box. The ornate wooden box. Diamond yellow and blue tiles coating it. Two circular gold handles. Three people beside it. She had no idea how they'd got it up here so fast. How they'd dragged it up the ladders. How they'd frigging got it inside Riversford unbeknownst to her in the first place.

"Are you ready, Martha?" Daniel asked, stepping up to the box.

He put a hand on the golden handle.

Started to turn it.

And although Martha wanted to shoot him, although she wanted to put him and his band of creeps down, she found herself nodding.

Saying yes.

"Good," Daniel said.

He turned the handle completely.

"Because what you're looking at right now is going to change the world."

He pulled open the door.

Martha saw what was inside.

Her knees went weak.

WANT MORE INFECTION Z?

The fourth book in the Infection Z series is now available.

If you want to be notified when Ryan Casey's next novel is released (and receive a free book from his Dead Days post apocalyptic series), please sign up for the mailing list by going to: http://ryancaseybooks.com/fanclub Your email address will never be shared and you can unsubscribe at any time.

Word-of-mouth and reviews are crucial to any author's success. If you enjoyed this book, please leave a review. Even just a couple of lines sharing your thoughts on the story would be a fantastic help for other readers.

For a full up to date list of all the author's books, head over to this link: http://ryancaseybooks.com/books

Printed in Great Britain
by Amazon